Sweet Nightfall

By Kathryn Vegas

Edited by Josh McCullough and Pam Anderson

Cover Photography by Jamie Suckow Photography

Cover Design by Paul Copeland

Cover Bracelet: Handmade by CelticLeatherWorks.com
Fenrir artwork by CelticHammerClub.com

Permission granted to the author to quote lyrics from the song Lump by The Presidents of the United States of America, by the rights holder Chris Ballew.

ISBN 978-0-578-61590-5 (Paperback)

For
My sweet family.
I love you dearly and forever.

Chapter One

Clark was always Sara's last resort fuck.

Why did I agree to do this again?

She was not feeling it tonight. There was no blood pumping through her veins, no quickening of breath.

Is this all I have to look forward to? Lackluster sex for the rest of my goddamn life?

Sara was thirty-nine and single.

That is not the spot!

Clark's moves left a lot to be desired. She seriously considered swatting his hand away. On extra lonely nights like tonight, Clark was a harmless way to be touched by another human being. In the past that was enough. Tonight it was not.

Clark had no idea his touches were not doing it for her. He was just happy to be there, bless his heart. Sara was a lovely woman.

They had been neighbors and friends for a decade. Every once in a while the stars aligned; she would drink the right amount, be lonely enough and he would be there to enjoy the hell out of it.

Tonight was one of those nights. Clark was stoked. His hand was between her legs performing a move he thought was driving her wild while he kissed her neck.

The lights were off. It could not be seen, but Sara's

face was thoughtfully bored. She systematically moved her hips to keep up the appearance of her participation. She was spiraling into a little drunken depression. She made an obligatory moan. His poking fingers were all wrong. If Sara and Clark had not been friends for so long she would have set him straight. Hurting his feelings was out of the question. He deserved to be touched and loved as much as she did. They craved human connection. Plus, she felt sorry for him. They were lonely kindred spirits.

Finally his poking fingers glided up to caress her breasts. He began to suckle.

That's better at least.

She rewarded him with a more sincere response. Sara reached around him to rub his soft back. Clark was in his late forties and wasn't one to exercise.

He's sweaty already?

Sara moved her hand away and wiped the wetness off on the sheets.

I've got to move this along. I'm not drunk enough.

She pushed him up and over. He rested on his side next to her trying to catch his breath. "I'll grab my vibrator and a condom, hold on." Sara reached between her bed and end table pulling out her trusty vibrator. She opened her drawer for the condom.

"You're such a good woman." He said gratefully. "I needed this. I'm glad you wanted to hang out and… and ummm… Then this."

Sara may not have been excited for this sexual encounter, but she was not one to miss out on an opportunity to orgasm. It was guaranteed with her vibrator. Tonight it was not happening any other way. That was certain. She knew what he wanted to hear.

"Just fuck me, Clark."

While he eagerly put on the condom, Sara got on all fours. She placed the vibrator between her legs and waited. Clark was out of shape and a good fifty pounds overweight, but at least he had a nice cock. He entered her from behind and hit the spot. Sara's pulse finally quickened.

"Oh god! Yes!" Clark was over the moon.

He bent over, pumping into her, his sweat dripped onto the small of her back. She ignored it and focused on her intention of getting off. She visualized herself being fucked by a virile, strong man. Her blood flowed in the right direction. Clark rested too much of his weight on her back. She was slowly being flattened.

Ignore it! Focus on the dick.

She kept herself on task, intensified her focus on getting off. She was now smooshed flat on the mattress. Her vibrator's buzz muffled against the bed. Closer to a climax she moaned from deep within her throat. Groans of her pleasure sent Clark into overdrive. He withdrew and drove back in again and again. Sara tightened all her muscles and held her breath. There it was. The extended pause. The splendid moments before the orgasm throbbed through her entire body.

Oh, thank god!

"I'm gonna come!" Clark grunted.

He stiffened and spastically jerked his hips. His full body weight smashed her into the mattress.

Good god Clark, you heavy bastard!

His belly and chest left her back soaking wet. She struggled to breathe. He finally realized he was smothering her and rolled off.

"Oh, sorry Sara. I got caught up in the moment."

"I just need… to breath," she laughed.

At least I came.

Sara clicked off her vibrator and tossed it back to its home. Clark rested on a pillow, his bald head shining with perspiration. His eyes closed.

"I'm going to wash-" Sara was interrupted by a soft snore, "off."

Sara sighed and climbed out of bed. She padded softly to her bathroom, flipped on the light and shut the door at the same time. Shaking her head, she walked up to the mirror and looked at her disheveled self.

"This is depressing," she whispered.

Clark's snoring drifted through the wall. She really didn't want to listen to him saw logs all night.

"Fuck." She whispered. There was no polite way to get rid of him. On nights like tonight, when things took this turn, he usually slept over. Sara's daughter was at her Dad's for the weekend.

I guess I'm sleeping in Hazel's bed tonight.

Clark was a great friend and neighbor. He was always willing to help Sara with any house projects. They spent a lot of time at school events for their kids. Clark was a widower and shy. He didn't date or make an effort to meet new people. The love of his life had passed away eight years ago. When things got extra lonely they would hang out, open a few bottles of wine and spend the night talking. It usually led to sex and happened every other month or so.

Sara ran water until it was warm at the sink and splashed her face. She gave her vagina a splash as well. She grabbed a towel, dried her face and wiped off the water dripping down her legs.

I need more than this.

Her options were limited and she knew it. She was thirty-nine with no prospects for a relationship in her life at the moment. Every good man she knew was married. The single men played the field with women a decade younger than her. How could she compete for men her age when twenty-five year olds would date them?

She frowned and shrugged at her reflection. Never one to wallow, she changed the subject and wondered aloud, "The important question now is, if there's any wine left?" A smile formed. "I think there is…"

She made her way quickly back to the kitchen.

Chapter Two

Of course Adam wanted to have sex with her. What man wouldn't? She was beautiful. Even though he wasn't actually a human anymore, he was still a man.

Kayla was twenty-three with a tight body. What Kayla lacked in personality she almost made up for with her perfect ass and she was very willing.

She thought herself a model. She was only 5'5" but Instagram didn't measure height. Adam popped a button on her designer silk blouse exposing a lacy black bra. Her breasts were full and perky. Held high and tight in a bra one-cup size too small. Her skin was an exotic caramel color, by choice or by birth he did not know.

Kayla looked down at herself. "Hold on! This is too good not to post."

Son of a bitch.

Adam was not surprised. She'd posted at least ten photos of herself and a couple live videos over the course of the evening. He had picked her up at eight and it was now around midnight. It had been a long night.

Kayla posed herself perfectly, pushing out her flawless cleavage. Her face at the exact angle she had perfected from years of selfies. *Click.* She checked the picture then moved onto the caption and hashtag. It took a few minutes. Adam waited next to her in the private VIP bathroom they had locked themselves into.

Oops. Oh my. That's a sexy wardrobe malfunction. #modelsofinstagram #sexybra #hotdate... Adam zoned out as she continued to ramble out ten more hashtags as she typed. She finally tapped post.

Kayla put her phone on the counter beside her metallic clutch. She turned back to him with a rehearsed apologetic smile, "Sorry but that was just like too sexy to pass up. My followers will drool."

She ran a hand down Adam's chiseled chest to his waistband. "Let's get back to where we were."

After this excruciating evening listening to her drone on about herself, if she was more than willing to have sex in this bathroom so was he.

"You are so hot! Every girl in this place was like totally jealous of me. We looked so fucking good together. Where do you work out?" She spoke in a monotone that was never truly interested in anything enough to show true emotion.

Adam didn't care how hot she thought he was.

She didn't actually wait for his response to her question. "You want to fuck me right now?" She pulled him toward her and leaned her face up passively for a kiss.

Good thing she's wearing six-inch heels. It brought her a little closer to his lips at his height of six foot four inches. He kissed her long and deep. He felt himself growing hard. Her hand caressed his erection through his pants.

"Impressive! Big Daddy." Kayla unzipped his pants.

Adam felt a bit of disgust forming in the back of his throat, but he was in it to win it.

She's smoking hot. Dumb as hell, but damn that ass.

He reached down behind her to grab a handful. Squeezing her nice round ass made him feel better. Kayla only saw him as a twenty-four year old version of herself. Beautiful on the outside was all she was looking for. Five of the selfies she posted tonight included him to show off what a good-looking man she could get. She didn't know he was really forty years old. He would look twenty-four forever.

It had been such a rough night listening to her. He was tired of being alone but he had no desire to ever put himself through this again. Since he looked twenty-four, the women he tried to date were his age physically but not mentally. They had nothing in common to talk about. Not that Kayla could really carry an intelligent conversation. She hadn't gotten a single joke he'd made all night.

Do real twenty-four year old guys want a girl like this?

She lifted her skirt to reveal a black silk g-string. She knew he could see her backside in the mirror behind them.

Oh yeah, I get it.

"That ass." Adam could not help but say.

"I know right?"

Kayla freed his erection. She played with his cock, putting it through the leg of her silk panties. Gliding the silk up and down the shaft while holding him against her warm skin.

The locked door handle jiggled as someone tried to open the door. Adam thought the jig was up, that he was not going to receive the bounty he was offered. The payoff to this horrendous evening might go up in smoke.

"We better hurry before someone like gets suspicious and unlocks the door." Kayla whispered.

Alrighty then.

Adam didn't have to be told twice.

Kayla positioned herself against the bathroom counter for the best viewpoint to watch her gorgeous self be fucked by this gorgeous man in the mirror.

She pulled her skirt up to her waist and bent over the sink. Kayla did not mention a condom. Adam, being immune to any human diseases, was not going to ruin the mood by pretending he needed one. She pulled her panties down and they whispered past her toned thighs to her stilettoed feet.

His cock was hard and ready. But first he just needed to worship that ass for a moment. He knelt down behind her. She laughed. It was not the first time a man had wanted to kiss her beautiful ass. Adam lightly nibbled and suckled at her plump checks.

If only I could get away with just one bite. He shook off the thought.

He couldn't help but think such things. He could only control that he did not act on his devilish thoughts. She shivered in delight. He smacked her ass for good measure, stood up and entered her swiftly.

"Oh, fuck yeah!" She squealed.

He pounded into her over and over. He let himself forget about the awful evening. Adam focused all his attention on the way her pussy felt. She was slick, warm and velvety soft.

"Unbutton your shirt!" She breathed heavily between words. "I want to see those abs while you fuck me."

Adam obliged.

"Oh my god, we look so fucking hot!" She reached down between her legs to tickle her clit. "YES!! OH fuck yes!".

Adam felt her tightening and pulsing on his shaft, pushing him over the edge. "Where do you want me to come?" he strained to say.

"On my ass!"

There it was. He pulled out and came all over that pretty ass.

Chapter Three

Sara pulled off the last of the wires attached to her patient's head. It was six in the morning. She'd had a long night of watching this little old lady sleep.

"Did you get any rest, Mrs. Elton?" Sara asked.

"Oh, I certainly did not. It was terrible. I was up all night with all these wires. I couldn't get comfortable at all," Mrs. Elton responded with a little extra morning grump than was called for.

They always said that, but Sara watched them all sleep for hours just fine on the monitor. She sympathized, "I'm sorry. I'm sure we got all the info we need and the doctor will diagnose at your next visit. You'll be sleeping like a baby in no time. Can I get you a juice or a water?"

"Yes. I'll take a cup of water."

"Go ahead and get dressed, use the restroom if you need to. I'll be back with water. We'll get you out of here and maybe you can go take a morning nap at home. Here is a form to fill out to rate your experience. Sign at the bottom to release the information to your primary care physician. Just leave it here when you're done."

Sara walked out and down the hall to a room lined with computer monitors and surveillance screens. Her fellow sleep technicians could be seen on the screens waking their patients.

"Ugh! I swear to God my guy farted all night long, so when I opened the door it was like a wall of fart I had to walk through to wake him up," Kelly announced as she walked into the private sleep technician's room. She mimed puking into the wastebasket by her station.

Sara laughed. "Oh shit. When I saw him last night I was like thank goodness he's not mine. I got the little old grumpy lady. Luckily her room was fart free this morning."

"I have the worst luck. Seriously!" Kelly shook her head, her face full of disgust like the fart still lingered in her nose. She sat down at her station and started inputting data.

Sara opened up the Uber app on her phone. She needed a ride home. She could have asked Kelly, they had been working together for four years, but she didn't like asking people for favors. There was one car available in the area. She requested a pick up.

Sara's daughter had turned sixteen last month and immediately gotten her license. The nights she was with her dad, Sara thought she should take the car. Her daughter, Hazel, had dropped her off at work on the way to her Dad's last night.

Sara filled a cup of water at the cooler and walked back into Mrs. Elton's room.

"Thank you," Mrs. Elton said taking the water from Sara.

"You're welcome." Sara picked up the filled out form and said, "You ready to get out of here?"

"Oh yes, I'm going to go home and sleep," Mrs. Elton yawned.

Sara walked with her out of the sleep clinic and rode the elevator down to the first floor of the medical building.

The area was empty this early in the morning. It was December and still completely dark. The air crisp and cold. An elderly gentleman in an old pick up truck waited at the curb. Sara helped Mrs. Elton get into the passenger seat.

"Good bye, Mrs. Elton. Have a nice day." She shut the truck door and waved.

Sara returned to the sleep clinic. She finished her paperwork and cleaned her workstation. An alert chimed from her phone to let her know her Uber had arrived. One last click to log off and she jogged out of the clinic, yelling goodbye to her coworkers.

It was dark and quite foggy. This time of year, the sun did not rise until 7:30 AM, which was almost an hour away. On the curb idling was a fairly new black Dodge Durango. She opened the back passenger door and hopped in.

"Hello there. I'm Adam." He turned around in his seat and looked over his shoulder at his passenger.

"Hello…" Sara was looking at the most attractive man she had ever laid eyes on. She recovered herself, "…I'm Sara, your extremely lucky passenger."

Sara giggled to herself like a schoolgirl. She smiled at him in disbelief. Even sitting, she knew he was tall. His broad shoulders took up more space than the width of the seat. His arm spread across to the other seat's headrest, muscles stretched the seams of his flannel shirt.

Sitting back in her scrubs, hair in a ponytail with no make up on, she knew because of her age she had carte blanche to flirt with this young man. He was as nonthreatening as a puppy and just as adorable.

Adam put the car in drive, "What do you do that you'd be leaving this early in the morning? Looks deserted."

"I work in the sleep clinic so it's the end of our shift

right now. We work from seven at night and we try to get out by six thirty but sometimes our patients are slow pokes in the morning. Luckily my patient was ready to get going right away." Sara explained.

"An almost 12 hour shift? That must be rough. How's working in a sleep clinic?" Adam asked. He pulled out of the parking lot.

"Boring. I stay up all night watching people sleep on surveillance like a creep. But I work alternating 3 or 4 nights a week. On the flip side 3 or 4 days off a week is pretty nice. How's Ubering?"

"It's not bad..." The first bars of "Lump" by The Presidents of the United States of America rocked from the sound system. Adam's hand jutted out immediately and turned it up.

"Haven't heard this in forever! I love this song! Did you profile me and choose a 90's alternative station?" She laughed and couldn't help herself but start in, "She's lump. She's lump. She's in my head."

Adam came in right with her, both knowing every word. They sang in unison to Sara's surprise.

"You know this one?" Sara questioned.

He kept on singing so she joined back in. Their duet was in perfect harmony. They were laughing by the end.

"That was awesome!" Sara laughed. "How did you ever hear that song enough to memorize it? You must have cool parents!"

Adam dodged the question, turned the sound back down and said, "There's nothing better than the Presidents."

"I really need to download that album for my daughter's Ipad."

"How old is your daughter?" Adam continued the

small talk as he maneuvered through the empty streets. Morning traffic had yet to begin. He took the freeway.

"She's sixteen. She has my car when she stays with her dad. Hence my need for you."

Sara's attention was drawn to his broad muscular shoulders, his long arm still stretched across to the passenger headrest. His profile was masculine with a chiseled jaw line. He smelled good too.

Mmmm, what a hottie.

Their eyes met in the rearview mirror. His green eyes were the color of peridot in sunlight. A jewel like green she'd never seen anyone have before. They shimmered in the light of the passing streetlamps.

Oh my… her mouth went dry.

"I bet you're a real lady killer? How many girlfriends do you have?" Sara joked.

"Only four or five." He winked at her in the mirror.

Oh man, I bet he's gay. She felt disappointment. *This guy could have any man he wanted.*

Adam continued, "In fact I went on a horrible date a few nights ago. This woman never put down her phone. She had a lot of followers I guess that needed to know what she was doing at all times. I'm not sure why."

Hmmm scratch that, not gay. Sara was inexplicably relieved.

"Oh man, what a dumbass. If I was on a date with a boy like you I would be all eyes." She winked back at him in the rearview mirror.

Oh my god, am I really trying to cougar it up with this kid?!

Fuck it. He's too cute not to. I'll never see him again.

Adam smiled, "Thanks. Obviously, she was not as

intrigued... but maybe her live tweet of our date was to imply that she was... I can't be sure."   In a perfect impersonation, "Umm but like yeah like I have like 10,000 followers on my IG account and like my friend has like 25,000 but for real she paid for them. Seriously! Just like trying to be better than me but like my followers are all legit."

Sara burst out laughing, "Oh my god! I can picture her. I'm sorry to laugh. That sounds horrible." She tried to make her face have a more serious expression.

He took the next exit off the freeway.

If only I was 22...

"She was horrible. I spent four hours with her. I'm pretty sure I became dumber myself by the end of the evening."

"You might have to buy a limo for your Ubering future." Sara laughed at her *Dumb and Dumber* reference.

Adam turned around quoted Lloyd Christmas, "This isn't my real job you know. My friend Harry and I are saving up money to open up our own pet store."

Sara was speechless for a second as she realized he got her joke and one-upped her. She cackled. Adam smiled at her and turned back around to watch the road. They entered her neighborhood. The ride was coming to an end too quickly.

"You seriously just quoted *Dumb and Dumber* to me? You are the best Uber driver I've ever had." She was still chuckling. "Were you even born yet when it came out? You seriously must thank your parents for making you so cool." Back to referencing the movie Sara continued, "You want to hear the most annoying sound in the world?"

"Always," Adam immediately answered.

"OMG like she totally copies me. Every time I post a

selfie she posts one like three seconds later. It's like ridic how much she wants to be me." Sara copied his earlier impersonation to a T.

Adam couldn't help but laugh at her spot-on mimicry. "Yep, that is the most annoying sound in the world. Looks like we've reached our destination."

Sara thought she heard disappointment in his voice but she dismissed it for wishful thinking.

Adam pulled into Sara's driveway. Her house was a quaint little bungalow with a front yard. The porch was decked out for Christmas. Her lights twinkled in the darkness of the winter morning.

"Your house is both charming and festive." Adam said

"Thank you! As you can tell I'm a big fan of Christmas."

She felt a pang of sadness that the ride was over. That was the most fun conversation she'd had with a stranger ever. Plus, he was a handsome devil. She tried to memorize everything about him to be able to tell her daughter later. The vehicle came to a stop and he put it into park. Adam turned in his seat with a smile on his lips. Sara put her hand up and rested it on his firm, manly shoulder.

"That was fun. Thank you." She opened her car door and exited.

"Yes, it was. Hope you have a great day and if you ever need an Uber again, I hope I'm available." Adam said out of his rolled down window.

"Me too!" She gave him one last smile, shaking her head at her own whimsical thoughts. "So dreamy," she whispered.

Chapter Four

Strong muscled arms wrapped around her body lifting her off the ground. She wrapped her limbs around his neck and waist. His hard cock enters her and fills her completely. His green eyes locked with hers...

OH god yes, that'll do it!

Sara held herself completely still and enjoyed the delicious build up. She sighed heavily as she let the throbbing between her legs pulse for as long as possible.

Oh thank you, Uber!

She smiled to herself. She felt satisfied and refreshed. She had napped after work for a couple hours and woke up to memories of green eyes. She could not resist a little midmorning masturbation.

"What a specimen. Damn." Sara sighed.

What she wouldn't give to be rich cougar material. She heard the front door unlocking, quickly clicked off her vibrator and threw it into its hiding place. She jumped to her feet and readjusted herself in the mirror. Sara looked into her flushed face and bright eyes and smiled. She walked out of her bedroom, down the hall toward the living room and entryway.

"Mom, I'm home!"

Sara walked around the corner, "Hey honey! How was Dad's?" They gave each other a welcoming hug.

"Good. Dad and Ben went out so I babysat. They came home at two in the morning. Really giggly." Hazel raised her eyebrows up and down and laughed.

"Oh that's great! Shawn needed a date night." Sara said. Sara and Hazel's dad Shawn had been best friends for twenty years. "How were your sisters?"

"Hellions those two, but they are so damn cute!" Hazel exclaimed. "Dad said to tell you that you owe him a cocktail and he wants to start living life again. The twins are a little less needy now and I've also proven myself to be such a good babysitter." They walked together to Hazel's bedroom.

"How much is he paying you?"

"Ten bucks an hour." Hazel smirked.

"Nice!" Sara put a hand up for a high five. Hazel obliged. Sara plopped down on her daughter's bed after knocking random teenage debris onto the floor to make room. "I need to stay up the rest of the day to get back on schedule. You want to go shopping with your new found wealth?"

"Of course I do. I can drive."

"Oooo we can get our Santa picture!" Sara exclaimed. Hazel rolled her eyes. It was a tradition that they took their picture with the mall Santa every year. No matter how old Hazel got.

Sara's eyes brightened, "Oh my god that reminds me. I swear this morning my Uber driver was the absolute best-looking guy I've EVER seen! Hazel. EVER!" Sara was very excited about this topic.

Hazel couldn't help but giggle, "For real, Mom?"

"For really real! I didn't see him stand up but he was tall. His shoulders took up half the front of the car! He had these eyes…" Sara got animated.

"Mom!" Hazel laughed.

"No Hazel for real. He had these sexy green eyes and his face! That face..." Sara trailed off like she was in a daydream.

"I've got to see this Uber man!"

"You would die. It was seriously like being driven by a movie star. He knew my kind of music." Sara stated.

"What?" Hazel didn't follow.

"90's music!" Sara nodded. "We totally busted out Lump, duet karaoke style."

"Busted a Lump?" Hazel had no idea what her mom was talking about.

"Oh my god child, give me your phone. I'm downloading the album for you right now. This guy must have had amazing parents and I've been a real failure having never made you listen to The Presidents of the United States of America!"

"Mom, you're so weird."

"Yeah, I know. It's my thing." She scrolled through iTunes, found what she was looking for and clicked purchase. "OK, there. Now your life will finally be complete and I can take back my Mother of the Year award."

"Thanks. I'm sure I'm going to enjoy this Lump thing." Hazel shook her head skeptically.

"You will, I promise. Oh that boy though, UGH! Heartthrob." Sara fell back onto Hazel's pillow, her eyes unfocused.

"This is the first crush I've ever seen you have. I mean like not a movie star but regular person in real life crush." Hazel contemplated.

"I wouldn't stand a chance with that 'regular person.' He was out of this world. Way too young for an old lady like me." Sara responded.

"You could turn cougar, Mom." Hazel's face turned thoughtful. She got excited about this idea. "When we go shopping today we're buying you cheetah print EVERYTHING!"

"Cheetah print?" Sara's brow dropped confused.

"Yes, it's like cougar dress code or something." Hazel replied.

"Okay, so you're the expert on cougar dress code?"

"Did you rate your ride?" Hazel asked.

"Oh shit I forgot." Sara pulled out her phone and opened the Uber app. It had a little picture of Adam. "Awww," She sighed. "He's so adorable!" Sara showed the screen to Hazel.

"O...M...G..."

"I know, right?!!" Sara exclaimed. "Five stars for sure! There's a leave a compliment option with choices, I'm going to click *Great Conversation*. It asks if I want to write a thank you note... Should I???"

"Yeah, you should!"

"What should I say?"

"You are super hot and thanks for the ride?"

"Umm no." Sara contemplated her options. "You were a very nice young man?"

"No mom that's a grandma thank you note."

"Ugh! Maybe I should skip it."

"No! Leave a note. Don't overthink it."

"What about, 'Thanks for the fun duet and hope you have enough for that pet store soon.'" Sara typed as she talked it out.

"What pet store?" Hazel shook her head.

"It was a joke we shared." Sara said in a dreamy voice.

She clicked submit. "Let's go. I feel the mall calling."

Sara hopped up and went to her bedroom to get ready.

Sara's bedroom was feminine. She had a flair for making things pretty. She checked herself in the dresser mirror, looking into her own eyes for a moment. She smiled but noticed the lines it made on her face. She leaned in closer and felt a pang of sadness.

Sara's smile faded as she noticed each flaw and the evidence of age. She had always been a pretty woman. She never really felt ugly or let herself dwell on such things. She had didn't have a problem with low self-esteem. She was confident about how fun she was as a friend and how she took care of everyone's needs. But now examining herself so closely was turning her normally joyful face into one she did not recognize. She leaned in even closer.

Am I pretty anymore? She noticed the gray in her hair.

When was the last time I dyed my hair?

She zoned in on her unkempt eyebrows.

How long have these been like this?

"I must need glasses," she said to herself and tried to smile. Sara hadn't put herself first in sixteen years.

"Why don't I take the time to spruce you up?" She asked her reflection.

"What?" Hazel asked from the bedroom door.

"I'm just thinking when was the last time that I took the time and effort to spruce myself up? I've felt stuck thinking and accepting I could never find a good man being the age I am. Men my age are married, or if single, date women a decade younger. Men in their fifties think they can date women in their thirties. And I'm about to age up into the forties. I just accepted those things as facts letting myself stay in my comfort zone. I say I don't want to be lonely anymore but have I really been putting the vibe out to the universe that I'm available?"

"Honestly, no Mom."

"If I ever want to attract a soulmate I need to be the best version of myself first and get out there" Sara nodded to her own epiphany. "And why haven't you told me my eyebrows are a disaster?!"

Hazel straight faced. "I thought you knew and didn't care."

"What kind of daughter are you?"

"A shit one I guess." Hazel said.

"And your dad?! Calling himself gay and letting the mother of his child go around with caterpillar eyebrows!"

Hazel could not stop laughing.

"Grab your coat you ungrateful brat." Sara laughed shaking her head.

Chapter Five

Shawn didn't knock. He used his key to open Sara's front door and swung it open to dramatically announce his arrival.

"Sara, I'm here! I know, I'm 30 minutes late so you have to be ready. Let's go!"

"I'm ready!" Sara announced and strolled around the corner waiting for Shawn's reaction.

"What the fuck?!" Shawn exclaimed in surprise. He automatically started nodding and walking around her appraising the new outfit and hairdo. "Yes! Yes! I love it!" Sara twirled around and Shawn clapped appreciatively.

"Thank you. Thank you." Sara posed and cocked her head sexily. She started laughing. Hazel was behind her smiling.

"Doesn't she look great?!" Hazel exclaimed, walking over to give her Dad a hello hug. They stood arm in arm contemplating Sara, looking at her with their matching brown eyes. "I picked out the cheetah print camisole."

"It's just the right amount of animal print. A little goes a long way," Shawn stated approvingly. Sara's new jeans flattered her long legs and hugged her butt just the way they should. The form-fitting jacket revealed a small amount of the silky camisole. "I can tell you didn't go to your normal discount store for those jeans. They are hot. Hmmm new pumps too. Nice!" Shawn paused for a second making a decision, "I'm not taking you to a gay bar tonight." He made it a statement.

"But I love our place." Sara said sticking out her bottom lip. "Everyone will love my new outfit."

"Yeah they'll love it. They'll give you lots of compliments but they will not want to take it off you." Shawn explained. "I heard all about your shopping spree and epiphanies from Hazel." Shawn exchanged a look with Hazel. "We're going somewhere with straight dudes tonight. Let's get your feet wet and maybe some other parts too. If we're lucky." He winked.

"Eww Dad, I don't wanna hear about Mom's wet parts! Jeez!" Hazel groaned.

"Go to your room then." Sara and Shawn said in unison. They looked at each other and laughed.

"I will." Hazel pretended indignation and stomped off smiling.

Sara laughed after her daughter and turned back to Shawn. "I miss you living here." She stated.

"I know, honey. I miss it too." Shawn said with a sad smile as he put an arm around her shoulders.

Shawn and Sara had lived together and raised Hazel until she was ten years old. Then Shawn met Ben, the love of his life, and moved on. Sara never moved on. She had been comfortable in their arrangement. When he left, she delved further into motherhood and work. He had been her roommate since the first day of college. They had become adults together.

Hazel was an accident. On a particularly lonely night after months of them both being single with no end in sight, they sought comfort in each other. They drank way too much that night. It had never happened before or after. Shawn liked to say that he blacked out and remembers nothing. Sara lets him say that. She always told the story that the fates were involved because Hazel was meant to be theirs. They both accepted Sara's pregnancy and created a beautiful, loving home for Hazel. She became their life.

"Oh I don't know. I don't want to go to a new place." Sara tried to find a reason to stick to the old familiar territory that was their gay bar for the last fifteen years. That place was safe. She didn't have to delve into new worlds there.

"Nope. Stop trying to think of an excuse to change my mind, you're living life tonight, bitch. Let's go!" He turned and walked back out of the house leaving her to follow or stay. Sara knew she had no choice but to follow.

Cocktails on the table, Sara and Shawn surveyed the sea of straight singles on the prowl. The bar was trendy and modern. It had opened within the last year. Everything that was currently fashionable was represented in the décor. Sara sighed, her inner interior designer knew in a couple years it would be completely dated.

"I don't think I'm ready for this." Sara said, a look of concern on her face. This place ended up being a little more meat market than she expected.

"We're just here to play tonight, to practice your skills. Don't worry. There's absolutely no one here I'd let you go home with honey. This is merely an exercise." Shawn reassured her with his judgment of the crowd. He could not hide the look of disgust on his face. That many straight people trying so desperately to hook up was unappealing to say the least.

"I can get behind that." Sara picked up her fancy looking cocktail and took a long drag. The memory of those green eyes sparked in her mind. Adam's eyes. Out of curiosity she surveyed the whole bar. Just in case.

"Who are you looking for?" Shawn could always read Sara's mind.

"A boy with green eyes and broad shoulders." Sara quipped. "He's not here."

"Hazel told me about Uberman. Is he your boy crush?"

"Oh you should have seen him." Sara said wistfully. She remembered his eyes framed by thick black lashes. She bit her lip as she daydreamed.

"What was his name and any personal details you remember?" Shawn held up his phone and swiped to start an investigation. Sara snapped out of her revelry. Shawn was a bit of an Internet sleuth. He could find out anyone's life details in seconds flat.

Sara was immediately onboard for this quest. "Adam. Unknown last name. He drove a black Dodge Durango, obviously works for Uber. Very tall, I mean I didn't see him standing but you could tell. He was just, oh so broad shouldered.... He had green eyes, dark hair, 24 or 25 at most."

"There's lots of Adam's locally but age narrows it down. Uber as workplace... We have 4 to choose from... OH and I can see which one is yours right away... OH my."

"Let me see! Let me see!" Sara exclaimed a bit too excitedly.

Shawn handed over his phone but they huddled together checking out Adam Holsten on Facebook.

"What a dish." Shawn stated. "You sure he's not gay?

He's too handsome and built to be straight. Oh if I was single..."

"Hey back off! He's my fantasy boyfriend," Sara laughed. "I thought that too but then after I asked him how many girlfriends he had, he told me about an awful date with a woman he had just been on a few days before. No, he's very straight. Very masculine energy like you just know he could rip your clothes off and throw you on a bed and..." She trailed off.

"You asked him how many girlfriends he had?" Shawn looked at Sara impressed with her outgoing nature. "That's hilarious!"

"I was just in scrubs with no make up. There was no pressure to be cool." She laughed. "He was young and way cute. You know me. I can talk and make jokes with anyone. But you know what's caught this kid in my head and become the source of all my masturbatory pleasure?"

"What?" Shawn chuckled.

"He was fun and silly. He quoted Dumb and Dumber back to me. We laughed together. Nothing makes me wetter." Sara smirked. "It made me realize I need that. I need a partner of my own. Hazel will be going to college soon. I need to cultivate a future for myself or I will be living in that house alone."

Sara paused scrolling down through Adam's photos. She could tell he was not a Facebook junkie. There weren't a ton of pictures but he'd been tagged in a few. Looked like he had very rich friends. He was tagged at a birthday party at what seemed like a posh restaurant. Everyone in the shot was dressed to kill. His gleaming white smile made her sigh. He stood out in every group shot like a beacon of strength and masculinity.

"Wow! Looks like he comes from money, but must be trying to make it on his own with the Ubering thing. Interesting." She scrolled through several more pictures. He was tagged in a few shots with the same beautiful people, always having fun and smiling.

Sara took a sip of her cocktail and contemplated what she would say next. "I want a man who is silly and fun and decently fit. Who doesn't smother me into the mattress."

Laughing, Shawn knew who she was talking about, "Oh, Clark."

"Yes, I'm done settling for Clark to fuck me because I'm so lonely. I settled for him for years now because he's harmless and nonthreatening. I want a man to snuggle on the couch with and watch old movies. I want to have amazing sex. I desperately want to have amazing sex!" She slammed her fist down on the table a little too hard making their glasses rattle.

Shawn nodded. "What are you going to do about it?"

"Well you know, I'm thirty-fucking-nine. Men my age... look at that jackass over there." Shawn turned to follow her gaze. A man in his late forties with bedazzled tight fitting jeans was chatting up a table of twenty something women.

"Oh, now that's sad." Shawn shook his head and shivered for dramatic affect.

"I know! Is that what I have to look forward to in this venture, douchebags and out of shape old dudes? There have got to be single men my age that are normal, that want to have a real companion in life. This place isn't a real representation of life, this is a hook up bar for sure." Sara took one last look at Adam Holsten's profile and placed the phone screen down on the table. Sara and Shawn started searching the bar for anyone that could be a candidate.

"What about that dude? Grey shirt, looks early 40's, fit, and has most of his hair." Shawn nodded in the man's general vicinity.

"Hmmm, not bad," Sara said contemplating him.

"Go up to the bar!" Shawn urged. "Finish that drink. Go up to the bar beside him, order another and be your normal friendly self."

Sara gulped down the rest of her cocktail. "OK. I'm going to do it. Its just practice." She stated.

"Just practice." Shawn assured her.

Sara stood up, straightened her posture and walked over to the bar. She sat on the barstool beside the man they had deemed suitable for such an interaction. He looked over at Sara and smiled. She smiled in return. Sara could tell he was game to talk to her, he turned his whole body toward her, ready to flirt. His eyes were a little too bright, a little too eager in Sara's opinion.

Give him a chance, he could be as lonely as you are.

"I've never been here before, do they have any noteworthy drinks?" Sara was a little disappointed in her opening line but that's all she could come up with.

"I just order beer so I couldn't tell you. I'm Kenneth by the way." Kenneth held out his hand to shake hers.

"Hello, Kenneth. I'm Sara."

The bartender arrived to take Sara's order. Before Sara could speak, Kenneth took over. "What's your most popular drink?"

"People love our Twisted Tequila Sunrise."

Before Sara could respond, Kenneth ordered one for her and made sure to let the bartender know it was on him.

Ugh, I don't even like tequila.

Trying to stay positive about this mingling practice, she

gave herself a pep talk. *Maybe he's just overzealous and thinking he's being cool. It's nice he ordered you a drink.* Sara tried to give him the benefit of the doubt but already dreaded having to drink it.

"Thank you, Kenneth." Sara said politely.

"You're welcome. You're too pretty to buy your own drinks." He looked at her through hooded eyes. She guessed he thought those were what they called bedroom eyes.

Sara was embarrassed by the compliment and the look was disconcerting. She contemplated pretending to become ill so she could just end this now. A silence fell between them for a moment too long.

"I thought I saw you sitting with a man?" Kenneth inquired.

"He's my best friend. We just wanted to hit up a new place. See what else the town has to offer" Sara replied. "Do you come here often?"

"So you guys aren't together?" He asked like he did not believe her. His expression said he had figured out something but Sara was not on the same page. "I got the vibe you guys are pretty close. Are you recruiting?"

Sara was perplexed, *recruiting what? I don't even know the dating lingo anymore.*

"Recruiting?" She asked shaking her head.

"You seem like a couple looking to add on to your night? If so, I just wanted to get past all the preliminary bullshit and say I'm in on the double team."

Sara's mouth hung open. The bartender sat her unwanted brightly colored drink in front of her. Sara, realizing her jaw had dropped, closed her mouth, clinking her teeth together.

"Thank you." She said to the bartender.

34

What the fuck have I gotten into and how do I get out?! Sara couldn't help but laugh at her predicament.

"I'm sorry, Kenneth. We've had a miscommunication; my best friend is gay and married. He's only here to morally support my entrance back into the dating world." She chuckled at this ridiculous conversation and took a sip of her awful drink.

"Even better. I'd rather not share if I don't have to" Kenneth looked her up and down.

"Actually, I better get back to him. He's been all alone a little too long. It was nice to meet you, Kenneth. Maybe I'll see you around." Sara desperately tried to politely, yet strongly, leave this awkward situation. Her creep meter alarm was going off. She stood up.

Kenneth realized he was losing and tried to backtrack. "Wait a second. Relax and finish your drink."

Sara was not skilled in navigating sticky social situations such as this. "Thank you for the drink. Really. I think I'm in over my head here. I thought I was ready but I'm going to have to gracefully back out of here. I'm sorry I wasted your time. I'm gonna go. Good luck tonight."

"Honey, give me your number. We can get to know each other. You won't be disappointed, I promise." Kenneth pushed like a car salesmen not taking no for an answer. "Come on. What's your number? I don't make the best first impressions. We can text. Please give me your number."

Sara felt trapped and all social conditioning not to be rude was warring against her desire to get away. Sara's consummate niceness also flared its head.

Maybe he really does just make bad first impressions. I shouldn't judge people so quickly.

She still planned on giving him a fake number; bad first

impression maker or not she was turned off by Kenneth.

"OK do you have a pen?" Sara asked. He smiled and held up his phone to program her number in.

Oh shit. I can't give him a fake number when he's going to immediately text me and see me receive it. Sara forced a smile and gave him her number which he immediately texted.

"Great, now we can get to know each other. Hope I get to see more of you soon." Kenneth seemed satisfied with himself.

"Nice to meet you. Have a good night." Sara had a bad taste in her mouth. She didn't know if it was the drink or Kenneth.

She headed back to Shawn with the most disgruntled look on her face. He couldn't help but laugh.

"What happened?" Shawn asked when she was seated beside him.

"That was Kenneth. He thought we were a couple looking to 'recruit' fresh meat for the night." Sara took a breath. "He was down to 'double team' me"

"Oh my god!" Shawn busted up laughing at her.

"Yuck it up." Sara giggled. "I told him to meet us at the car."

Shawn laughed even harder at her joke.

"Ugh he has my number. I couldn't get away! You don't write down fake numbers on napkins anymore for creeps!" She put her face in her hands, shaking her head.

Sara's phone alerted her to a text message. She turned over her phone and swiped to come face to face with a big, veiny cock. "What the fuck?!!"

"Dick pic?" Shawn assumed.

"How did you know?!"

"Honey, we invented the dick pic. Show it to me!" Shawn said, loving the drama of the evening. He was having a blast tonight. Nights like these with Sara had been few and far between since the twins were born.

Sara looked up to see Kenneth giving her a salute and a smile. She awkwardly gave a disgust laden half smile back and looked away as quickly as possible. She pushed the phone over to Shawn.

"Oh man, that's veiny." He said shaking his head.

Chapter Six

Adam pulled over to the curb in front of an upscale nightclub. Attractive, well-dressed people littered the sidewalk laughing and flirting with each other, waiting to be let inside. They sparkled in the light of the streetlamps. Light reflected off their bling, sequined dresses and glittered shoes. The back door of his Durango opened and a passenger slid gracefully inside.

"Hello Adam." A familiar voice said as she shut the door.

"Rebecca." Adam said frustrated. "What are you doing?"

"Don't get testy, Adam." Rebecca's voice was smooth as silk. "I'll play fair."

Adam turned around in his seat to look her in the eyes. Rebecca was as beautiful as she was deadly. Her aura was powerful and sexually charged. She seemed to look down on everyone.

She stared back at him, her amber eyes shined with intention. Ageless, she looked exactly the same as the first time he had seen her. She took his breath away sixteen years ago. Now he was more objective. Yes, she was utter human perfection on the outside but on the inside there was no humanity left. Rebecca waited for him to speak.

"What are you doing?" Adam repeated.

"I'm just checking on you, baby." She purred.

"I'm fine. Thank you. No need to pay for the ride. You can get out and be on your way."

"Take me home, Adam. You don't want a one star rating, do you?" She smirked.

"I know what you think of my lowly life choices, but can you keep the condescending tone to yourself?" Adam conceded and turned back around. He knew he had no choice but to complete this ride to be rid of her.

"I'll never understand why. You had it all."

"According to you, not me." Adam stated.

"According to everyone. How many people would die for what you were given?" Rebecca shook her head.

Adam pulled away from the curb and hit the gas.

Might as well speed this up and get her home quickly. They rode in silence for a few miles.

"I miss you, Adam." She said earnestly breaking the awkward silence.

Adam was almost lonely enough to say it back. Almost.

"When are you coming back to me?" She raised her hand up and ran her fingers along his muscled shoulder.

"Rebecca, I haven't changed my mind." Adam stated. He accelerated onto the freeway.

"I worry about you. Are you staying fed? If you need help with that you know I can make sure you get a stockpile while you play human."

"I'll take care of myself my way, but thank you." In no way could he become beholden to her again. It was tough to live an honest life while being driven to drink blood to survive. He could use a stockpile, but not from her. Rebecca's gift would come with a price beyond the deaths of those she drained. Adam could not wait for this ride to end.

He remembered the last time he'd seen her, when he'd finally walked out the door. The look of disbelief on her face was almost comical. She knew she was one of the most beautiful women in the world. As an Elder vampire, the power she held was palpable. She never considered he would ever really leave.

Fifteen years he'd spent with her. His maker. He was an impressionable twenty four year old when she waltzed into his broken life. The life she offered was opulent. Her eyes promised pleasure. She introduced him to her world of grandiose wealth and it was amazing to be powerful and timeless. She offered an easing of his painful loss.

Adam's parents had recently died in a car crash. He was an only child. His world had fallen apart. Rebecca offered a new life: companionship, a new home and a way to move on when he felt lost. Adam felt a sudden pang of sadness.

"Rebecca, I'm sorry. I'm not trying to hurt you. You have given me so much. It was an amazing adventure, but I'm not in love with you anymore. I'm not in love with the lifestyle we led. I want to live an honest life. I know I can take anything I want from any human, but I don't want to murder or steal. I want to make a life like my Dad's. I want a loving, modest home. Maybe figure out how to raise a couple kids with a woman that loves me like my mom loved my dad. I want be part of a family, not a coven. I want to earn a living, make a normal life."

"You're not human, Adam." Rebecca stated the obvious.

Adam, frustrated, ran his hand through his hair. "I know that, Rebecca."

"You are my mate. I chose you to spend eternity with

me. We belong together."

"I know you think that. I understand, but maybe there is someone else out there that would love to spend eternity living the life you want, but it's not me."

"You'll come back to me. There is no human life for you. What do you think will happen when you find this paragon of a woman and she finds out you're a monster? I love you for who you are."

Adam didn't respond. He feared that every day, but he was still going to try to find a soulmate, a partner to laugh with the way his parents laughed together every day. He grew up in such a happy home. Since their death he'd had no home. He lived with Rebecca, but their house was not home. He had lived alone now for almost a year and the emptiness of his house was beginning to wear him down. All he wanted was to feel that feeling again. Contentment.

Adam exited the freeway and made his way down familiar roads to the home he had shared with Rebecca. He turned into a gated community, rolled down his window and put in the code to open the gate. The heavy wrought iron swung silently open. The houses were spaced far apart with well-manicured lawns. Each estate was nestled perfectly into a couple of acres. The community was built with a French countryside inspiration. In the dark you could see into each home through their oversized windows. Their crystal chandeliers shimmered as he drove by. The road curved around another beautiful villa.

"Don't you miss this?" Rebecca asked.

"Of course, it's an amazing place to live, but there's more to life."

Rebecca rolled her eyes.

Adam turned into the next driveway. The landscape

was lit to perfection, showing off the trees and shrubbery that lined the driveway. He pulled up to the entrance, a ten-foot tall double door imported from a derelict French castle. It's wrought iron accents added to its impressiveness. One human could never open one of those doors on their own. It was as much a defense mechanism as it was a design element. Adam put the car in park and waited.

Rebecca moved in closer behind Adam and firmly ran a hand down the front of his chest. She whispered in his ear. "Come inside, Adam. I've missed you in my bed. You can go back to your human life tomorrow. A human woman can't take your full strength like I can. You have to miss being able to fuck the way a vampire can fuck."

Oh, man. Stay strong. Adam struggled with himself.

"You know I can take anything you dole out, baby." Rebecca practically purred in his ear.

You have got to get out of here.

Adam grabbed her hand to stop its descent. Rebecca's lips brushed the side of his neck. He could feel himself hardening.

Resist! He took a deep breath and pushed the hand back over to her.

"I'm sorry. It's not happening." He wanted to say it firmly but by the end, his voice caught. He knew she could tell she'd gotten to him. She chuckled.

Fuck.

"Alright. Tonight I'll let you go, but if you get hungry for it, you know where to find me. I can satisfy you in ways *they* will never be able to and you know it." She opened her car door and stepped out. She slowly walked around in front of the car. Her silk dress billowed in the wind and clung to her body with every step. She wore no undergarments. Her breasts only covered by a layer of red silk. Adam groaned. Rebecca smiled but did not turn back. She seductively stalked her way to her front door and opened it with ease.

Adam breathed out heavily once the door shut behind her.

You did the right thing. Shake it off.

The memory of that delicious body of hers riding him hard, meeting his every thrust...

Stop. Cancel. Put the car in drive and go, you dumbass!

The drive back to his place was long and depressing. It seemed now to be a cramped neighborhood of small houses with tiny, neglected yards. Adam pulled into his garage feeling defeated. He clicked the garage door to close.

Who am I kidding! I can never have the life I want. What normal human woman would want to have a family with a fucking vampire? You're so fucking stupid!

Adam felt his anger growing with each moment. His breathing was erratic and the familiar thirst reared its head. He knew he needed to calm himself down. Going into a rage right now could hurt innocent people. They didn't deserve what he could do if he were to ever lose control.

Just breathe. She got to you. It's all right you have eternity to find The One. Rebecca is wrong.

Adam slowed his breathing and concentrated on hope. He focused on the first memory of his parents that popped up; Christmas when he was eight years old. He'd watched the video of that Christmas so many times, that the memory was ingrained like it was yesterday.

He was wearing Spider-man pajamas when he ran downstairs to see what Santa had brought. His mom's hair disheveled, as she held the camera capturing the moment.

His dad stood beside her smiling with a bulky VHS hand held camcorder on his shoulder. That year Adam had asked Santa for the Nintendo Power Pad set with the zapper gun. Santa had never let him down, but he was prepared for disappointment just in case. He'd heard that parents were fighting over them at stores and they were hard to find. Adam slowed down as he approached the Christmas tree.

The tree was twinkling with strands of multi-colored lights and dressed with handmade ornaments. Every ornament he'd ever made with clumsy kid hands hung proudly from the branches.

"What do you think, buddy? Did Santa come through?" Dad asked. Adam's dad was larger than life, where Adam got his height and broad shoulders.

"I don't know, Dad." Adam said worried.

"Start opening, sweetheart." Mom said. Her kind face and big green eyes looked at him adoringly.

Adam didn't want to go for the bigger looking present first. He didn't want to seem greedy and what if it wasn't the Power Pad. He excitedly began to open a present labeled "from: Mom and Dad" while his parents enjoyed watching his joy.

"RAD!" Adam exclaimed over an Optimus Prime Transformer.

"You like it?" Mom asked, even though it was obvious.

"It's awesome! Thank you!!" Adam ran over and hugged her. Dad's camera followed him, capturing mom in all her morning bed head glory. She made a face at Dad and motioned for him to get the camera off of her.

"Keep digging. Let's see what else is under that tree." Dad exclaimed, smiling.

Adam decided to take a chance on the big one that

was labeled "from: Santa." He had a strong suspicion it was the Power Pad set. He looked up at his parents. They looked back at him almost as excited. He tore into it like a wild animal.

"YES!! OH MY GOD!" Adam yelled. "Santa got it for me!! LOOK!! MOM! DAD! LOOK!!" They of course were already looking.

"Wow buddy, you must have been good this year!!" Dad zoomed in on Adam's happy face, chuckling at his son's amazement.

"That's so cool!" Mom was always supportive.

"Can we hook it up now?!!" Adam asked excitedly.

Tears rolled down Adam's face as he sat in his garage reliving one of his favorite memories. A smile remained on his lips as he pictured his mother running on the Power Pad while unbeknownst to her, Dad had the camera rolling. Her hair wild and curly, wearing her pajamas, she tried her best to beat Adam in the race. They were both laughing as she started losing, but her competitive nature was strong. She dropped down to her knees and cheated by using her hands to hit the pad's buttons faster than her feet could ever run. Dad was laughing his head off in the background. She won the game.

"No fair, you cheated!" Adam was appalled.
Mom rolled on the floor laughing, then looked up to see Dad had been recording the whole time. The memory of her shocked face made Adam laugh out loud. It always did.

Chapter Seven

Sara stood in front of the mirror inside the sleep clinic's employee bathroom. She'd finished her shift and had sent her patient home. No longer wearing her scrubs, she was dressed in her new jeans and a fashionable V-neck t-shirt. Her chestnut hair was down, full and thick, hanging past her shoulders.

Hazel dropped her off last night. It had been a week since her ride with Adam. She'd thought of little else since, especially at bedtime. Sara had obsessed her entire shift over requesting an Uber to take her home this morning. Would it be Adam? To be safe, she had played out all possible conversations in her mind until she had worked herself up into a basket of nerves.

Sara applied a new lip-gloss and inspected herself.

I'm looking casual, not too fancy, but not Plain Jane in my scrubs.

What am I doing?!

I'm not doing anything. I just want to see a cute boy. That's all. It's no big deal.

He's so out of my league. What am I thinking?

I just want to see his pretty face! I can do what I want!

Sara grappled with herself.

She grabbed her phone off the counter, tapped the Uber logo and requested a ride before she could talk herself out of it.

Adam had time for one more ride before dawn. He opened up his Uber app and made himself available. Within a couple minutes he got a notification. It was the sleep clinic again. He remembered his rider from last week. She was a cool woman. The Dumb and Dumber joke on the five star review she'd left him was cute.

He accepted the ride and arrived at the clinic 10 minutes later.

The chilly winter breeze burst through the open door. She smelled of vanilla and something very earthy, a subtle spicy fragrance. Adam took a long breath in to enjoy it.

Sara hopped in the back of the black Durango. Her hair bounced around as she got comfortable and put her seat belt on. He hadn't noticed before. It was a rich chestnut color that curled at the end. She was wearing a thin, loose fitting V-neck t-shirt that showed off her cleavage. Her hoodie was open. Adam had an urge to take care of her and zip it up.

"Hello again," greeted Adam.

"Good Morning." Sara replied as she shut the door, "Brrrr! It's so cold!" Rubbing her hands together she cocked her head to the side questioning, "This seat is awfully warm though, was it vacated recently?" She laughed.

"I remembered to turn on the seat warmer for you." He turned around to look at her.

"Oh my goodness! This is nice!" Sara exclaimed as she sunk down low into the seat absorbing it's warmth. She put her hands under her thighs, "Ahhh yes!" She exaggerated.

Adam chuckled. He enjoyed watching her make a big deal about the warm seat. She found joy in little things. It was cute, and so very human.

Adam put the car in drive and made his way out of the parking lot. The sky was still black in the early morning. The few cars left in the lot were frosted over.

Sara's heart was beating fast. Adam could hear the blood pulsing through her body. This combined with her infectious joyful demeanor, conjured thoughts of drinking from her and sharing her vibrant life-force. He was used to such thoughts and knew how to quickly cancel them. Luckily, he had already fed tonight and could easily swat away bloodthirsty thoughts.

She seemed nervous as the silence lagged on. Adam watched her in the rear view mirror as he stopped for a red light. The red illuminated her face in the darkness. Her big blue eyes expressed uncertainty.

Why is she so nervous?

On some level can she tell I'm a monster?

Is she frightened?

Sara hesitantly broke the silence. "Is it okay with Uber if you drive us through the coffee shop I like?" He watched her bite her lip awaiting his response.

"Of course. Which one?" The light turned green. Adam glanced back to see her satisfied smile. Her eyes sparkled with excitement when he passed under a streetlight.

Why that look in her eyes?

Hmmm. Maybe not scared, but attracted?

Is she trying to make this ride last longer? Interesting.

"Cool! Thanks! About two blocks more on the right. My friend owns it, so I try to support her whenever I can." Sara explained. "There it is, Sweet Beans." She pointed to the little freestanding coffee cart sitting in the middle of a parking lot.

"You're friend owns a bikini girls coffee drive thru?" Adam questioned.

"Yup!" Sara smiled knowingly. "You're going to love it!"

"I'm sure I will," Adam replied nodding.

Adam pulled into the empty strip mall parking lot. The little drive thru stall was lit up like a Christmas tree. The sign flashed "Sweet Beans! We get you going with espresso and eye candy." It had pull up windows on both sides. Adam pulled up to the window that was free.

"What would you like to order?" Adam asked.

Sara hit the button to roll down her window. "Oh when they see me they'll know." She smiled at him.

The young woman inside saw the Durango pull up. Her jaw dropped a little when she caught sight of Adam in the front seat.

Sara had to call attention to herself, "I know, right?!" Sara said. The barista's big eyes turned toward Sara. Understanding each other immediately, they both raised their eyebrows at each other and started giggling. "Stacy, this is Adam, my extremely super handsome Uber driver." Sara winked at Stacy.

Adam shook his head at the ladies and good naturedly rolled his eyes.

"Nice to meet you, Adam." Stacy struck the cutest pose, leaning out of the window to show off her lovely cleavage held only by a string bikini. Her skin immediately covered in goosebumps, her nipples erect.

Sara laughed at Adam's awkward silence.

"I want my usual. Adam your drink is on me. What do

you like?"

Adam finally got his voice back, "Black coffee. Thank you."

"Anytime. How's your morning hon?" she asked Stacy.

"It's going pretty well. Fun customers and good tips. Now you and Mr. Uber are here. You look cute this morning, by the way." She raised a perfectly manicured eyebrow at Sara and went to work on their drinks.

The customer at the opposite window drove off. The second barista waved eagerly at Sara and stared at Adam before she started helping Stacy with the drinks. The two young women giggled and whispered to each other.

"How's the coffee here?" Adam asked Sara, lacking any other suitable thing to say.

"Hit or miss." Sara shrugged with a laugh. "But the baristas are always on point," She said as Stacy bent over to pick up a cup she dropped. From their vantage point in the Durango, they didn't miss an inch.

"I can see that." Adam replied with a smile.

Sara chuckled. Stacy handed Adam a black coffee.

"Thank you." Adam said.

Sara handed Stacy a ten and indicated for her to keep the change.

"You're so sweet. Thank you!" Stacy gushed.

"How are finals going?" Sara asked.

"They are killing me!" Stacy dramatically exclaimed. "I spent the whole night finishing a paper. Fell asleep at two, then had to be up at four to be here. I'm like dying right now. Why are you Ubering?"

"Hazel has my car while she's at her dad's. She dropped me off. It turns out to be a win/win situation." Sara cocked her head in Adam's direction.

"It sure is." Stacy agreed.

The second barista finished Sara's drink and handed it to Stacy.

Adam couldn't wrap his head around the familiarity and friendliness of these bikini clad baristas and his passenger.

Maybe she's a fun lesbian?

But her eyes told him a different story every time they happened to meet in the rear view mirror. She seemed a bit embarrassed every time he caught her eye and would quickly look away.

Stacy put a couple chocolate covered espresso beans on top of Sara's drink and handed it out to her.

"Thank you, sweetheart! See you later. Have a Merry Christmas, Mister Uber!" Stacy said as Adam pulled away. Adam rolled up both their windows.

Sara held her drink with both hands and took a sip. "Ah yes, this morning is a hit."

"Good. I'm glad." Adam smiled at her in the mirror. Sara looked into his eyes and audibly sighed. He watched her contented face for a few seconds.

Adam could smell her coffee. It was sweet and nutty. The smell of coffee and hazelnut mixed deliciously with her own vanilla fragrance.

"You should go back when you're not on the clock and see if Stacy is free for a date," Sara said. "I know she's not seeing anyone. You already have being gorgeous in common."

Adam raised an eyebrow as he turned back onto the main road. "Does she have an Instagram following?"

"Yes…" Sara hesitantly said.

"I'll pass." Adam responded. "I'm done dating young

women with followers to please."

Done with young women... but not women...

Adam's brain started mulling over this new revelation. *I haven't tried actually dating women that are my real age.*

He looked in the rearview at Sara enjoying her coffee with abandon. She closed her eyes as she sipped, her face reflecting pure pleasure. Adam felt his body respond to the expression on her face. He imagined her lying on a bed underneath him with that expression.

Whoa, buddy. Calm down.

He readjusted his position in the seat to take the pressure of his jeans off of his dick.

Sara sipped her delicious hazelnut latte. She knew she was going to regret drinking it since she actually needed to nap when she got home, but getting it was her only idea to make the ride last longer. She mulled over what he just said. *"I'm done dating young women with followers to please."* What could she say now? She knew what she wanted to say.

How about giving an older woman a try? What I could do to you boy.

Oh my god, you are being crazy. He's twenty-four years old! Don't embarrass yourself.

She opened her eyes and caught him staring at her in the mirror his green eyes inquisitive. Awkwardly she averted her gaze.

What the hell was that? You have to get this back on track. Be witty.

"Okay so no more Instagram models." Sara racked her brain for a segue to another topic. "Look at you, you don't need any dates set up by an old lady like me."

Sara could tell by his reaction in the mirror that he didn't like what she had said.

Crap. Pull it together!

"...I tell you one thing. I've never had a better view of the baristas than in this Durango." She said tapping the leather seat beside her. "It's like I'm looking down on the world. I'll never forget how she picked up that cup she dropped."

Adam started laughing, "I was beginning to question if the car payments were worth it. But after this morning they are."

"Damn right it's worth it!" She exclaimed. They both laughed together nodding their heads.

Whew! I righted the ship. God, I'm good.

"I was a little surprised to drive through a bikini coffee place this morning. I'm sure their clientele is mostly male. You said your friend owns it?" Adam asked.

"Yep. I've known the owner for a decade. She's great! I support women no matter what they wear. It's female owned and operated and those girls are paying for college. You better believe I don't mind handing them my money. And another major plus; I get to admire the ladies. Mmmmm." Sara trailed off remembering Stacy leaning out the window.

Oh, what I wouldn't give to be Stacy's age again. I would grab this boy and never let go.

Adam turned onto the freeway. She knew she had about nine minutes to spend with him. She prayed for gridlock. She longingly looked at his broad shoulders. His hair was grown out past his ears. He had it tucked behind them. He smelled so good. Masculine and earthy.

Sara imagined crawling into his lap and snuggling in front of a fireplace. She finally remembered one of the talking points she had gone over in her head last night a hundred times.

"After our first ride I went straight home and downloaded The Presidents onto my daughter's phone. I caught her trying to play "Peaches" on her guitar yesterday!"

"Nice!" Adam replied. "If you want to start a Presidents cover band, let me know. Cause we have "Lump" down pretty good already."

Gulp. Was that an invitation for an outside-of-Uber meet up??

NO, you crazy old lady! He's being nice!

...Whatever. A girl can dream.

You seriously think he wants to start a cover band? Sara argued with herself.

"You're right. That one's in the bag," Sara responded, nodding her head. Adam smiled back at her. His eyes were kind and genuinely friendly. Sara forgot what she wanted to say next, letting several moments of silence pass. "Do you play an instrument or will you be the lead singer?"

"I used to play the drums in high school, so if that's like riding a bike I could pick up the sticks again." Adam replied.

"No no no. We can't have you behind a set of drums. That would be a waste. You're frontman material." Sara stated. "You're our ticket to mega-stardom."

"Really?"

"Oh, yes. I would ride your coattails to fame and fortune." Sara stated.

Dude, I would ride your coattails so hard. She smiled to herself. Talking to him was so invigorating.

Sara's phone chimed a notification. She found it in her purse and checked it. Hazel had texted. *Did you get to ride with your green eyed boyfriend?* Sara chuckled. Adam looked at her in the rearview mirror.

"My daughter wondering if I got to ride with the cute driver I told her all about." She answered his curious look honestly.

Why did I tell him that? He's gonna think I'm a creeper.

Adam shook his head and smiled.

Sara texted back, *I'm in the car with him right now!*

"It's pretty early in the morning for a teenager to be awake." Adam said.

"She's got a little part time job she needs to get up and get to this morning. She's a very independent, responsible girl. She's saving money so she can pay for half of her own car and won't have to borrow mine anymore. Her dad and I told her that we'd match her dollar for dollar." Sara felt a rush of pride talking about Hazel.

"Well, I hope she doesn't save too fast. It's nice driving you." Adam said.

"Aww, thanks. Don't worry, it'll take her a while to save enough on minimum wage." Sara felt warm all over. She didn't know if it was the warmed seat or her body overheating from being in a confined space with so much masculine energy.

Her phone chimed again. Hazel texted, *Are you wearing any cheetah print?* Sara smirked and threw her phone back in her purse to ignore her.

"It seems like you raised a pretty good kid." Adam said.

"I think so, but I'm her mother and I think she's perfection made real. I bet your mom loves to show you off."

Sadness entered Adam's eyes. He said wistfully, "She did."

Sara immediately felt the shift in energy.

Oh, no. What? He said, "did."

"I'm sorry. I didn't mean to say anything that would make you sad." She scrambled to apologize.

"Don't feel bad. Don't worry about it. I shouldn't have said it like that. I should have just gone along with it. I'm sorry. It makes people really uncomfortable to talk about stuff like that. I had a wonderful mom. We were a very close family. They've been gone for a while now."

"They?" Sara asked dreading the answer.

"My mom and dad were in a car accident. They passed together... a few years back."

Sara felt crushed for him. It broke her heart. She tried to control her breathing as her eyes began to tear up.

Adam shook his head. "Man. I did not mean to..."

"Stop. Don't apologize for anything. You can tell someone something sad and it's okay. I'm really sorry that happened." Sara said as a tear rolled down her cheek. She didn't want to bring attention to herself, so she concentrated on slowing her breathing and not sniffling.

"Thank you. You're a very sweet person. Let's talk about something else. We can't end the ride on that note," Adam said as he pulled off the freeway.

Sara wanted to hug him and never let go. She controlled her urge to cry and got her emotions under control. He pulled into her neighborhood and she wracked her brain for a way to end the ride on a positive note, but she couldn't think of one.

"I see you've added more lights to your Christmas display," Adam said breaking the silence. Her house could be seen from further away than the last time they rode together.

"Oh yes!" She said. "I think it's as Christmas as I can get it now."

"I love it. Good Job! It's very Clark Griswold of you."

"Thank you!" Sara was proud of her Christmas display. "My electricity meter is spinning just as fast as Clark's did. My bill is scary as hell every January."

"I bet it is."

"It's worth it, though. It makes me happy." Sara stated.

Adam pulled the car into her driveway surrounded by colorful lights and Christmas cheer that lit up the interior of the car like daylight.

"Thank you for another great ride, Mr. Uber." Sara said.

"No, thank you. It was a pleasure." Adam said turning around in his seat to look at her.

The full force of his attention on her made her lose her breath. "Damn, you're so fucking handsome!" Sara turned red. "Oh god, I can't believe that came out of my mouth." She started laughing. "I think, though," she said waving her hand in front of herself. "I'm at the safe age that I can say whatever I want, so there. I've decided that. So I won't go home, replay this in my head and want to die for the rest of the day."

Sara opened the door to escape the awkward moment she had created. The brisk morning air rushed into the car. She hurried out of the car and shut the door before she could embarrass herself further.

"Sara!" Adam's deep masculine voice called out to her from his rolled down window. She turned around, her hand on her heart. "I wanted to wish you a Merry Christmas in case I don't see you again before the holidays."

"Merry Christmas to you, too." She waved at him, shaking her head at herself as he reversed and drove away.

Chapter Eight

The sky was beginning to lighten. Sunrise was fast approaching. Adam needed to get home as fast as possible. He drove with speed and precision out of Sara's neighborhood and back to the freeway. He took too much time driving her home. He was enjoying himself so much he had not been his normal cautious self. He had driven slower than usual, and stopping for coffee had taken more time than he had that morning.

He replayed the ride in his head, going over every detail of their conversation. She was so full of light. She was his age but would never know it. An older woman would never see him as a potential husband. He knew from the way Sara's body reacted to him that she was attracted to him. By calling herself an old lady, he knew she didn't see him as a potential boyfriend.

Adam could not help but think of the possibilities. He actually had things in common with her. She grew up through the same decades that he had. The girls he'd been dating had never heard of the bands he liked or the movies he grew up on. They had so many shared interests. She was a pretty woman. He was definitely interested in her sexually. He remembered her face as she passionately enjoyed that latte.

He let his mind drift to images of her passionately enjoying his dick. It was an easy image to bring up. A woman with that much joy for life had to be a fun lay.

He remembered her face when he'd mentioned the death of his parents. The single tear that slid down her cheek. The way she silently slowed her breathing to control herself. Her reactions were so honest and raw. He could hear every heartbeat acceleration. He could feel her empathy for him and it was genuine. He could kick himself for mentioning that. He shook his head.

I'm supposed to be driving people like a professional, not telling them my sad sack story. Now she feels sorry for me. She probably thinks of me like an orphaned puppy.

The impending sunrise filled him with dread. It reminded him fully of what he was; a night creature, a monster. Sara was daylight and he was night. He wondered why he kept kidding himself, by playing human. She was a woman so full of warmth that she made a dark December morning feel like a bright summer day. He felt human during the ride with her. She made him laugh. The banter back and forth was easy.

He pushed the Durango to ninety miles per hour, passing by slower vehicles as he raced down the freeway. He checked every angle for any police. Minutes later he exited the freeway and felt safer being close to home. He could relax a little as he swiftly made his way through the familiar streets of his neighborhood. He breathed out a sigh of relief when he clicked his garage door opener.

The door slowly rose, revealing two stilettoed feet, connected to long legs standing in the doorway to his kitchen.

"Rebecca." Adam groaned. He pulled the car into his

spot and turned off the engine. He sighed and shook his head before getting out of the car.

"This is what you left me for?" Rebecca asked. "A twelve hundred square foot box in a low end neighborhood? To drive people around and pay bills?" She threw a handful of Adam's mail to the ground in disgust.

"It's thirteen hundred, thank you. I want to live the life I would have lived. I have eternity. So spending a while playing human isn't the end of the world. I really don't understand why you are acting like it is," Adam replied. He walked toward her and picked up his mail while she glared down at him.

Rebecca looked completely out of place in his modest home. She was wearing the latest designer fashion and shoes that cost over a grand a pair. Diamonds reflected light from her ears and neck. He looked her up and down. Only a vampire could look this exquisite.

"What made you risk being caught by the day?" Rebecca asked. "I'm worried about you. You would never have been so careless before."

"I had an interesting ride." Adam countered. "You don't need to be worried. I'm a forty-year-old man inside here. I can take care of myself. Speaking of which, you better get going before..." He cocked his head toward the open garage door.

She shook her head. The sun was about to rise. Adam knew she had no choice but to leave. Adam heard a car pull up. It was Rebecca's blacked out Land Rover.

"I'm flying to Garda tomorrow to spend Christmas in the Villa. Everyone will be there, of course. There's a ticket on the counter if you would like to join us." She stated. "I still love you. Please consider coming. You can continue this farce after the holidays."

"Tell Joe 'hello' for me," Adam said, referring to her driver.

Rebecca didn't reply as she walked out of the garage and entered the backseat of the Land Rover.

Adam watched it drive away. He pushed the button on the wall. The garage door closed off the entering morning light.

"Goddamn it." He muttered to himself.

Adam entered his kitchen and spotted the airline ticket on the counter. Christmas was two weeks away. The worst time of year to be alone. He was dreading its arrival.

He missed his parents so much. Growing up, Christmas was his favorite holiday. After their passing, he at least wasn't alone. Rebecca had taken him in and made him part of a coven. He had spent Christmas in a lavish villa for the last fifteen years. It was populated with vampires that had known each other for hundreds of years. They made sure to get together each year to renew their friendships and catch up with each other. They had welcomed Adam with open arms. After all these years, he considered them his closest friends.

He pictured himself spending Christmas in this house all by himself. He took a deep breath and tried to shake off the depressing scene.

I'll just drive people. I'm sure they'll feel sorry for me and add onto the tip. At least I can make some money.

That's even more depressing. Driving happy people to and from family events on Christmas.

What choice do I have?

...Go to Italy! It would be better than sitting here alone.

No.

Adam shook his head. An image flashed in his mind of Sara standing with her hand on her heart amongst the glittering of thousands of Christmas lights.

I bet her home is filled with love at Christmas.

He wandered into his living room and turned on his TV and Xbox. He wasn't ready to go to sleep just yet. He felt antsy. This wasn't as easy as he had hoped it would be. He thought it would be simple to find a human that would fall in love with him. He was not stupid, he knew what he looked like. Human women had fallen over themselves to be with him all through his teenage years and early twenties. He'd always had girlfriends. Then Rebecca came along, he had spent fifteen years with her. But he still saw the looks and sexual attraction in the eyes of other women.

He didn't realize that in fifteen years he would mature and become a grown man and the women in their early twenties were still the same. Now he was stuck in this body but his mind wanted more than the young women he dated had to offer.

Could Sara think of him as anything but a boy?

Worse than a boy. Now she thinks I'm a sad, motherless boy. Fuck.

He knew he could find women his age to have sex with him but would they ever go against social norms and commit to a relationship with him?

He opened up Netflix. The first rows of options were all Christmas movies. National Lampoon was right at the beginning, reminding him of Sara's Christmas light display.

He smiled shaking his head. He wondered what the inside of her house looked like? Does she bake holiday goodies? Adam hadn't really bothered with human food since leaving Rebecca. They would dine at the most exclusive restaurants but never ate while at home. He could still enjoy human food. It just did not sustain his life. Since the break up he had refrained all together. Why bother, he couldn't cook anyways. But thinking about a home-cooked holiday meal prepared with love, made his mouth water.

Does she have a boyfriend? That thought rubbed Adam the wrong way.

Hell, she could already be in love with someone. I know nothing about her.

Adam grabbed his phone from his pocket. He knew a thing or two about how to find out about someone. He put her address into Google to find her full name. Sara Hartford.

"Ok Sara Hartford, who are you?" He mumbled to himself.

Within a few clicks he had her Facebook profile. Her big blue eyes and the smiling face of her profile picture greeted him. She was posing with what had to be her daughter on Santa's lap. Adam almost laughed out loud. They had the same hair color and smile but the girl had brown eyes. They looked happy.

Scrolling through her posts, he could see that she was passionate about feminism, gay rights and advocating for women's health issues. She had a lot of friends and was tagged in photos smiling and hugging them. One man was good looking and they were smiling and posing together in a lot of the pictures together. He had brown eyes and looked a lot like the girl.

Must be the dad. They seemed to be best friends. *That's really odd. Why are they not together then? Oh…*

The next picture was the dad with another man, Sara's daughter and two toddlers posing in color-coordinated outfits.

What's the story here? Adam read all the captions. He learned that Shawn was Hazel's Dad. He was gay but also Sara's best friend.

Did she use him as a sperm donor? That's very progressive. Maybe there's no competition on the scene.

Adam spent the next thirty minutes scrolling through all her pictures and then moving on to scrolling through all Shawn and Hazel's pictures. He checked out any other social media accounts linked to her name and smiled when he found her Instagram account. It only had 42 followers. He mulled over all the new information.

Not only a Vampire, now I'm a stalker too. Good god. He made fun of himself and threw his phone aside.

Chapter Nine

Hazel barged through the front door.

"Mom!"

"I'm right here." Sara yelled from the couch where she was scrolling on her phone.

"How was your boyfriend?" Hazel teased.

"He was as dreamy as ever." Sara replied and turned off her phone. "Oh! Poor kid lost both his parents in a car accident a few years ago. It was just the saddest."

"Oh no! That's terrible." Hazel said, her face filled with sympathy.

"I know! I nearly lost it! It breaks my heart… Poor thing. Seriously like…" Sara choked up and could not finish her sentence.

Hazel walked over and landed beside her on the couch. Sara grabbed her up in a bear hug.

"I love you my Hazelbug! Have I told you that enough?"

"Umm yeah like a hundred times a day for sixteen years. I think it's been enough."

"I haven't been able to get that out of my head all morning. I couldn't take my nap to get back on schedule from thinking about it. The coffee I made him drive thru and get me didn't help."

"So… you took him to Sweet Beans?!" Hazel raised her eyebrows.

"It was the only thing I could think of to extend the ride." Sara sheepishly replied. "Now it's too late for a nap. I just have to stay up the rest of the day. So… I'm going to grab coffee #2 and hit the gym."

"The gym again, huh?"

"That's right baby. I'm gonna get in shape!" Sara said, flexing her muscles.

"Good for you, Mom!"

"I also need to wear those cheetah print work out pants you made me get." They laughed together.

"Uh oh, cougar alert!" Hazel joked.

"I'm on the prowl!"

"But what about Mr. Dreamy Green Eyes?" Hazel asked.

"Mr. Dreamy Green Eyes is a pipe dream sweetie." Sara patted her on the head like she must be simple minded.

"You always told me anything is possible." Hazel jumped off the couch. "Believe it and achieve it. Dream big! You can make your own reality. You are a Goddess in human form! Visualize what you want and manifest it. Don't stop believing oh oh OH!" Hazel dramatically repeated back all the mantras she'd heard throughout her life ending her rant in song. Sara laughed and rolled her eyes.

"Yes. Yes. Yes. Thank you. I won't stop believing. I'm sure I will continue spending time visualizing about a night with Mr. Uber." Sara paused with a sigh. "In the mean time, I'm also going to go to the gym and look for a dude my age."

After a long work out, Sara walked up to the dry sauna. She wanted to sweat out some toxins. It was a co-ed sauna, which meant there could be available men inside. She took a deep breath and opened the door.

She was greeted by oppressive heat and one shirtless, entirely too hairy, old fat man. The sweat poured off his face and dripped through the carpet of gray hair on his chest. He looked up at Sara and smiled.

"Sure is hot in here." He stated. Sara nodded and smiled back at Captain Obvious.

She took a seat at the opposite end of the long bench. The heat surrounded her. It actually felt good to be in a room so warm when the weather outside was so cold. The gym had been a bust for meeting anyone so far, but at least she was on the path to self-improvement.

Sara leaned back against the cedar planks and closed her eyes. She envisioned Adam in the front seat, his long muscular arm draped over to the passenger seat. His face turned around to look at her. His masculine jawline and hair tucked behind his ears. Those green eyes sparkling like faceted gemstones. Sara smiled. She heard the door open, pulling her out of her daydream.

A forty-something man walked in. A *fit* forty something man. Sara assessed him quickly. He had short black hair, silvered at the temples, cut like a businessman. He was shirtless, post workout. He was well built and obviously spent a good amount of time at the gym. No wedding ring, but could have taken it off to workout. He was handsome, with a dark five o'clock shadow that was sprinkled with gray.

Shit, this kind of forty something guy is still out of my league. Fucking stupid men dating younger women.

Sara shrugged and gave up on the day.

"Whew, it's hot," Captain Obvious again, this time to the newcomer.

"Sure is," The newcomer politely responded. He chose to sit on the second level of seating nearest to Sara.

"I think I've reached my limit. Have a good day," The old man said.

"You too." Sara and the new man said in unison.

Laboriously he got to his feet. Sweat dripped from everywhere. He stiffly made his way out of the sauna in slow motion. The door shut behind him. Sara was alone with the handsome shirtless businessman. She glanced over and saw two bare masculine feet beside her. His ankles were hairless up to mid calf, rubbed off from years of wearing socks. His feet were well maintained, nothing disgusting or overgrown.

"Haven't seen you in here before?"

Is he talking to me?

Sara looked at him confused, but his eye contact confirmed he was indeed talking to her. Also she was the only one left in the room with whom to talk.

"I just started going to this gym last week. I usually don't come this time of day but I ruined my schedule with a coffee this morning. I have to stay up the rest of the day." Sara realized without some backstory this answer made little sense.

"I'm a sleep technician. I stay up all night watching patients sleep. I should have taken a nap when I got home this morning, but I dumbly drank a coffee. I have three days off. So, I need to get back on regular people time. I'm Sara by the way." She rambled wishing she had said, *yes I'm new here.*

"It's nice to meet you Sara. I'm Steve. Don't people usually wait until after the New Year to start working out?" He asked congenially.

"Well I decided I wanted to put myself out there, you know? Starting to take care of myself was first on the list." Sara replied.

"Put yourself out there?" He inquired with a raised eyebrow.

Sara was a little embarrassed to admit that she was looking for a man.

"Um well, out there in the dating scene."

"Oh…," he trailed off.

Yeah… "oh…" is right.

Sara shook her head. I need to escape this and never come back to this gym before noon again! Sara brushed a sweaty tendril of hair from her cheek and took a deep breath of the smothering air.

The silence loomed as thick as the air.

"How have you liked it here so far?" Steve asked.

"It's pretty nice." Sara responded quickly, happy he broke the silence and was still talking to her. This was good practice for future interactions with men. Not wanting the conversation to lull again she asked, "How long do you usually stay in this." Sara indicated the room with her hands.

"I usually try for twenty minutes but generally wuss out at fifteen," he chuckled. "They keep it around one hundred and seventy degrees. On a good day when I'm hydrated, I can meditate and enjoy the heat. On a bad day it's like sitting in hell."

"Which is it today?" Sara asked.

"Well you're taking my mind off the heat, so it's definitely not hell today."

"Glad to be of service," Sara quipped. She had almost forgotten the heat herself except for the river of sweat cascading between her boobs. She was impressed with how well this back and forth was going.

"I told you what I do for a living, can I ask what you do out in the world?" Sara didn't want the conversation to end.

Maybe just maybe I can cultivate a chance with this man if he could see my sparkling personality.

Sara knew she still had to find out if he was married or seeing someone.

"Do you think you can guess?" Steve asked.

"No." Sara laughed. "I doubt I would guess right."

"What? Give it a try." He coerced.

"Well." Sara said reluctantly. She wondered why this guessing game. She wasn't really a fan. "Since you're only wearing workout shorts and there isn't a single clue to go on... I'm gonna say proctologist?" She smiled innocently. He smirked.

"You are bad at guessing."

"Maybe it's the heat. Or maybe I've never been good at guessing games." Sara responded. She was not used to sitting in a sauna. Her heart was beginning to pound in her red hot ears. Sara did not know how much longer she could sit there and talk to this man even if he was handsome and could possibly be a contender. She took a deep swig out of her water bottle. The water had been heated by the room and was not exactly satisfying.

"Alright maybe the guessing game was a bad idea and it built up an expectation of my job actually being exciting." Steve shook his head, seeming a little embarrassed. "I'm basically a traveling salesman or a client entertainer with an expense account." His expression reverted back to confident swagger. "I guess I'm new to this." He paused a little too long.

"New to what?" Sara was wildly guessing in her head.

"I hope this isn't too forward?" Steve began. Sara held her breath. She didn't know what he was about to say. "You said you were wanting to put yourself out there. Well I'm recently single and looking to do the same. What about putting yourself out there with me Friday night?"

What?!! Is the Universe granting wishes today?!

"Really?" She couldn't help but say and immediately wished she hadn't. "Uh I mean... Really?" Sara sighed.

Wow, Sara. Just wow, so smooth.

"Yes, Really." Steve laughed, his confidence shining in his eyes.

"That sounds nice." She said nervously.

"Good." He smiled showing very white teeth. "I can pick you up at eight? What's your number? We can text the details later.

Sara gave him her number. He entered it into his phone and texted her right away. She had not brought her phone into the sauna, so she would have to respond later.

The flush of adrenaline and the heat of the sauna was making Sara lightheaded. She needed to exit as gracefully and quickly as possible.

"Well Steve, it was nice meeting you. I look forward to putting myself out there with you Friday." Sara stood up and sweat dripped off her face. "I would shake your hand but I feel rather gross and drippy."

"We'll save it for Friday." Steve agreed.

"Have a good day," Sara said for a lack of anything better to say and left Steve in the sauna.

Sara walked back to the locker room in an overheated daze.

Did I really just get a date???

Oh my god, I really just got a date!

Sara's brain frantically concocted all manner of reasons to worry. She hadn't been on a date in so long she couldn't even remember. She was going to be alone with a stranger for an entire evening. She was already nervous.

Unless he's a creep, then I'm out. She reassured herself and nodded.

Oh shit, what if he's a creep? Why would he ask me out?

Because I'm a good looking woman and he could sense I was nice.

How could he tell you were nice in the minutes it took him to ask you out. What's his game?

Shut up, I'm not going there. I'm assuming he's a good man and the Universe is on my side.

Sara's inner monologue was in overdrive. By the time she got to her locker she was so consumed with scenarios she forgot in which locker she'd put her things. She stood around drawing a blank for several minutes.

Get yourself together!

Chapter Ten

Adam sat in his Durango on a dark side street, not too close and not too far away from the sleep clinic. He had made sure to be available every morning since his second ride with Sara. She had not requested another ride in almost a week. He was beginning to think he was crazy yet he continued to wait.

He was sure today would be the day. He knew she needed a ride this morning. He had watched her get dropped off by her daughter last night. He knew it was creepy when he did it.

He had to be careful, a vampire's penchant for obsession could be uncontrollable. With all senses heightened and a predator's instinct, there was a strong call to hunt. Hunting for prey or hunting toward a goal was all the same and it could overpower all other thoughts.

He could not stop himself from daydreaming about her. The memory of Sara's infectious laughter rang like a bell in his head. He was certain this was the key to his dream of a normal life. He had to see if he could date a woman his actual age.

Could a woman his age take a relationship with a twenty-four year old looking man seriously? He didn't know.

Would an older woman ever introduce him to their family as a serious love interest or would he just be a fuck toy. He definitely would not mind finding that part out with Sara. The image of her face enjoying the latte flitted across his mind and morphed into her on top of him. He imagined the ways he could make her smile.

"Goddamn it." He muttered to himself and picked up his phone. He turned off his availability. It was past the time she would have needed him. "I've got to get over this," he said aloud to his empty vehicle.

Sara had spent a little too much time chatting with her coworker Kelly about her impending date tonight. She was excited, but also avoiding the fact that she needed a ride home. She had the strongest desire to see Adam again. She knew it was crazy to think about him and long to see his face, but she couldn't help it.

You have a date with a very handsome man tonight, be satisfied!

Steve had left on a business trip the day after she'd met him at the gym. They had texted back and forth throughout the week. Steve texted her every night. It was nice. She was looking forward to this evening.

"I've got the whole day planned. First, I need to get home and sleep. I want to feel good tonight. I bought a special bath bomb. You know the ones that are like throwing a ten-dollar bill in a bath and watching it dissolve. Shawn is going to come over while I get ready and Hazel is going to do my hair." Sara excitedly went over her to do list with Kelly.

"You Ubering home?" Kelly asked. She pulled her coat off her chair and put it on.

"I don't think so. What if it's Adam again, two rides was fun but a third? I don't want him to think I'm some weird old cougar trying to get on him." Sara said. "That would be pathetic. The two rides were perfect and I don't want to ruin it. It could spoil the memory and the fantasies I've been enjoying."

"Do you want me to drop you home?" Kelly asked.

"That would be really nice! I should have already asked you." Sara didn't like being a burden on anyone. She was going to have to figure out what to do now when Hazel had the car, continuing to be Adam's rider would be too weird.

"Naw, it's cool."

Together they clicked off monitors and pushed in desk chairs. They waved bye to other coworkers on their way out.

Kelly was ten years younger than Sara. She was a robust woman. You could tell she never turned down beer or pizza. She spoke her mind and did not seem to be afraid of anything. Kelly was interesting and dramatic. She made staying up all night a little less boring for Sara. They had a great dynamic, finding humor in most anything. Both of them had potty mouths and dirty minds.

"Where is Mr. Businessman taking you tonight?"

"A little place on the other side of town. It's called Alder Lounge. I looked it up. Top shelf cocktails and such. Had good ratings. You been there?"

"Nope, never heard of it. Does it look like I go to top shelf cocktail bars?" Kelly laughed. "All I need is happy hour at a tavern. Get a couple of cheap beers and a few well vodka tonics. Dive bars always have tater tots. You know how much I love tater tots. I bet Alder Lounge don't even serve tots!" Kelly made a face at Sara that said what a mortal sin that was.

"Oh my god, I bet you're right. Fuck that, if there's no

tots, I'm out!" Sara joked.

They both shivered and wrapped themselves tighter in their jackets when they opened the door and stepped out into the freezing morning air.

"Fucking BRRRR!" Kelly yelled into the dark, empty parking lot. "I hate winter! You think you're gonna get laid tonight?"

"It's definitely on the table." Sara said. "We've been texting every night and they have gotten pretty flirty, on the verge of sexting."

"That's some serious shit!" Kelly laughed. She opened the front driver's side door of her old Jeep Wrangler. She climbed in, leaned across and manually unlocked the passenger door so that Sara could get in. Sara hopped in and put on her seatbelt.

"I know. I'm so nervous! I haven't had sex with anyone new in so long!" Sara laid her head back on the headrest and closed her eyes.

Kelly cranked up the Wrangler and flipped on the heater. She bounced in the seat trying to get warm. She shivered loudly. "Sorry, it takes this beast a few minutes to heat up."

Sara missed the heated seats of the Durango and the delicious looking man who drove it. "It's ok." Sara opened her eyes. The windows were completely frosted over. It was going to be a few before they could see out the windows.

Kelly reached over and opened the glove box in front of Sara. It was jammed full of papers and random junk. She rifled around grabbing a lighter and a little tube container.

"Do you wanna smoke?" Kelly presented the joint like a sacred offering.

"Oooo Nice! Why thank you, madam" Sara smiled. She

was just planning on going straight to bed when she got home, this would probably help. She had been afraid with all the anxiety over her date that she wouldn't be able to sleep this morning, which could ruin everything. She did not want bags under her eyes or to be too tired to get sexy if the opportunity arose.

Kelly lit the joint and took a long drag. Held it and breathed out a plume of pungent smoke. She coughed. "Oh that's good shit."

She handed it to Sara. Sara did the same. They each took one more turn before Kelly returned the joint to its tube.

The windows were finally clear of frost, but the inside was smoky. Kelly rolled down her window to let it out. Sara's head felt heavy. At least she was not worrying about that date anymore. Her mind drifted.

"Did I tell you about that Uber driver's green eyes?" Sara asked.

"Yeah, you mentioned those."

Kelly rolled her eyes at Sara good-naturedly.

"They even sparkled in the dark. Like gemstones." She laughed making fun of how Sara had described them.

"Shut up!" Sara laughed. She sighed, "They really did."

Kelly put the Wrangler in drive and left the parking lot. Sara's head rolled back and forth with each bounce of the suspension.

"I don't know how you function high? I seriously can't do shit but lay down when I'm stoned. I can barely talk right now."

"You're just a little bitch I guess." Kelly joked. They both laughed loudly.

Sara grabbed her phone out of her purse to check for

any notifications. Nothing. No new texts from Steve. He was flying back to town today from Phoenix. She scrolled for a second on Facebook to make sure she had not missed anything. She put her phone back in her purse. "What are your plans for tonight?"

"It's date night," Kelly said excitedly. "Dropping the kids off at my folks' house. I'm hoping to get nasty with Jared in an empty house. The kids are fucking driving me nuts and it's only a few days into Christmas break."

Kelly and Jared had started their family early. At twenty-nine she already had a ten and eight year old. Sara had met Kelly's kids a few times and she believed they could drive anyone crazy. Those two boys of hers were constantly roughhousing. Sara could only handle it for a few minutes before becoming anxious. Kelly was a rough and tumble woman. Sara imagined her man-handling Jared tonight and it made her smile.

"Does Jared have a safe word?" Sara poked fun.

"Safe words are for pussies," Kelly said with a sneer, which made Sara crack up laughing.

"Poor Jared," Sara said, shaking her head.

"Poor Jared my ass, that fucker loves it!" Kelly replied.

Sara's imagination swirled with visions of what Kelly and Jared's sex life might be like behind closed doors. She could see Kelly as a dominatrix with Jared in a ball gag on his knees. Now that would be interesting to see. Sara always wondered about what other people were doing in private. Her vibrating, stoned brain was flying around picturing all kinds of depravity poor old Jared could be enduring.

Sara could feel her heartbeat.

Fuck I'm so stoned right now. Am I being weird? My hands feel weird.

Sara raised her hands and looked at them.

Oh my god does that seem weird that I'm looking at my hands? She's never going to smoke with me again if I'm weird.

"It's really good weed, huh?" Kelly had seen Sara contemplating her hands.

Sara couldn't help but start laughing which made Kelly laugh. Sara decided to be quiet for the rest of the ride and keep her hands in her lap.

Chapter Eleven

It was four o'clock. Sara was lying in her bathtub. She had bought one of those shimmering luxury bath bombs on a whim and it was worth every penny. It was pink and covered in fine glitter. It was so feminine and extravagant. The smell of jasmine and clary sage seemed to penetrate her pores. She had prepared her space carefully with candles and her favorite crystals.

This was a ritual bath to bring out her inner Goddess tonight. She wanted to feel beautiful and be completely uninhibited by any insecurities. This was her chance to put herself out there, to find a partner. Even if Steve turned out not to be it, she would at least give it her all. It would be good practice for the real deal, she told herself.

Her hair, already washed in the shower earlier, was piled up on top of her head, ready to be styled. Sara was visualizing herself as her best self tonight. Her eyes closed. The pink tinted water lapped against the back of her neck. She loved that sensation. Anything delicately touching the back of her neck always made her shiver with delight.

Sara's mind wandered from tonight's date with Steve to riding with Adam, her go-to fantasy lately for personal gratification. She bit her lip imagining his broad shoulders.

Those emerald eyes glittering in the rearview mirror. The seams of his shirt straining against his biceps. The sharp masculine jaw topped with those kissable lips...

Damn it. Cancel. Cancel. I'm not going on a date with a boy tonight. I'm going on a date with a man. A man in my own age bracket. Stop it.

Sara remembered Steve's silver streaked hair. How unfair a man's graying hair is culturally accepted as distinguished, another level of sexy. She made a face.

I bet all Steve does to get ready for a date is shower and dress.

Sara's phone chimed. She sat up and shook off her wet hand before she grabbed it off her bath caddy.

It was a text from Steve, *Hey beautiful. I'm back in town and can't wait to see you tonight. Pick you up at 7. Text me your address.*

Hmmm. Hey beautiful, huh? That's nice. Oh, please be fun tonight. Please let the stars align for me.

Sara replied with her address and a smiley face emoji. She placed her phone back down and laid back in the steaming pink water with a sigh.

She loved the big claw foot tub. It was deep and long with golden claw feet. She had renovated the master bathroom herself after Shawn had moved out. Sara loved making things beautiful. She had splurged on this tub and turned a boring master bath into a feminine oasis.

Bright white wainscoting encircled the room with a light and airy teal blue-green paint on the walls above it. She accented the room with splashes of royal purple and hibiscus pink. The rugs were fluffy and white. She spent so much on the tub, she ended up having to tile the floor herself. She was very proud of this bathroom. Sara spent a lot of time soaking in that tub, usually with a glass of wine or two.

Sara heard the front door open and close.

"Who is it?" She yelled out.

"It's me." Hazel answered.

A few seconds later, Hazel walked through the bathroom door.

"Pink bath bomb? I'm hoping." Hazel asked.

"Yes a very luxurious fancy bath bomb. It was freaking like ten dollars to just dissolve in my bath water. I'm one fancy bitch."

"You certainly are. Are you nervous?" Hazel questioned.

"No. Who me? No. Yes." Sara smiled.

"You'll be great. Everyone loves you." Hazel assured her.

"Thanks, honey. You're sweet to me."

"Dad said he'd be here by five. He said getting ready was the best part and wouldn't miss it."

"Good. I need all the emotional support I can get." Sara said.

"I'm going to leave you to your luxuriously overpriced bath and go make a sandwich. Love you."

"Love you too." Sara closed her eyes and listened to Hazel's footsteps head toward the kitchen.

She's such a good kid.

Sara wrapped herself in a soft fluffy robe. Her skin felt silky and she smelled divine. She smiled and hugged her favorite robe around herself. She was still nervous for the date tonight, but she'd centered herself in the bath. She was ready to take on this new chapter like the strong confident woman she was.

Sara walked into her kitchen where Hazel was sitting on a barstool enjoying the last bite of her sandwich.

"Do you have any plans tonight?" Sara asked.

"The gang's gonna come here since you'll be gone?" Hazel's smile said please.

Sara rolled her eyes. Hazel's "gang" was two sweet gay boys and her best friend Jessie. They were pretty sweet kids who so far hadn't gotten into trouble. Sara had watched them grow up together since the second grade.

"Are they spending the night?" Sara asked. Hazel clapped. She knew that question meant she could host a slumber party, independent style.

"Thank you! Thank you!" Hazel jumped up and hugged her Mama.

"I'll be texting all their moms to let them know I won't be here so they can yay or nay their own sixteen year old coming over here unchaperoned."

Hazel was still smiling, she knew they would all get to come. Her friends lived in the neighborhood and their parents could easily walk over and check on them, so it was no biggie. Having the house to themselves with no parents was going to be awesome.

"I don't know when I'll be coming home or if I will. Are you ready for this responsibility? This is a big deal. If you do something weird to break my trust tonight the next two years until you're eighteen are not going to be as fun as they could be honey. You understand? I don't want to even worry for a second tonight about what you're doing."

"Mom you know us, and you know their parents will be doing drive-bys and pop-ins. We're just excited to have a house to ourselves."

"OK," Sara pulled her phone out of her robe's pocket. Opened her text messages and scrolled down to the last time she'd communicated with the gang's parents. She texted, "FYI the kids want to hang out here tonight because I won't be here. I have a date. I don't know how it's going to go or if and when I'll get back. There's a key under the door mat for any surprise check ins." She tapped send. The mothers of Hazel's pals were all good friends with Sara. They had ended up spending a lot of time together over the years since the kids were so close. "There."

"You're the best!"

"I know, right." Sara joked. "If you need a parent tonight for any reason call your dad."

The front door opened. "Speak of the devil." Sara quipped.

"Hello! Where are my ladies?!" Shawn yelled from the foyer.

"In the kitchen." Sara yelled back.

Shawn rounded the corner holding out a grocery bag. "I bring snacks and champagne for this momentous occasion!"

Sara clapped, "YES! Let's get me sexified and a little buzzed!"

"God, I love this dress." Sara said as she lifted the glass of champagne and saluted herself in the mirror. "I spent too much on it, but damn. It's just cut perfect. I've never felt as pretty as I do right now. Hazel, you did amazing on the hair. Thank you, sweetie."

Sara turned around to look at Shawn and Hazel lounging on her bed. Her green dress swirled gracefully around her legs. She drank the last bit of champagne.

"That dress will knock his socks off." Shawn said.

"I hope more than just his socks." Sara winked.

"Mom! Gross." Hazel shook her head.

Sara spun around to look at herself some more. Her blue eyes sparkled in her reflection. "Thank you, Mr. Uber." She said out loud.

"What?" Shawn asked.

"Mr. Uber, Adam was the catalyst for this. I would not be standing here in a designer dress feeling like a beautiful woman about to go on a date with a handsome man if it weren't for meeting him. He must be my guardian angel."

"I'm so happy you are happy." Shawn said. The guilt he carried for leaving her alone after he had met Ben had always lain heavily on his heart. Now seeing her shining so brightly, he could see she was ready to grab life again. His eyes began to mist up.

"Guys!" Hazel saw the impending teary scene. "Don't get mushy. Mom will mess up her makeup."

"OK. OK. I'm pulling it back together," Shawn said waving his hand in front of his face.

"It's just a first date and it's OK if it's the first of a few first dates. I'm ready for that." Sara said.

The front door bell rang. "He's here!" Sara sounded like a teenager. They all smiled.

"Should we hide in here or come out and meet this Steve?" Shawn asked.

"Come out. I would never hide you guys!" Sara grabbed her dress coat and handed it to Shawn. "Hold this. I don't want to put it on until he's seen me in this dress." They all walked to the door. Sara took a deep breath and opened it.

Steve stood on her porch with a bouquet of fresh flowers. He had a confident smile on his handsome face. His five o'clock shadow sprinkled with silver flecks that seemed to sparkle from the reflection of the Christmas lights on the porch.

"Hello Sara. You look amazing!"

"Thank you! Come in. It's freezing!" Sara in only her dress gestured for him to hurry inside so she could shut the door behind him.

Steve looked around him and spotted Shawn and Hazel. "Hello, I'm Steve." He put his hand out to Shawn.

"This is my daughter Hazel, and her dad. My best friend, Shawn."

Steve didn't miss a beat or seem concerned, "Good to meet you Shawn. Hazel, you look so much like your mother." He shook both their hands.

Shawn gave Sara a look of approval. Sara smiled back at him excitedly. Steve turned back to Sara and handed her the flowers.

"That's so thoughtful, thank you. Hazel, can you put these in water for me? You remember what we talked about. Make good choices." She handed Hazel the flowers and gestured for Shawn to help her put her coat on. Sara buttoned up the front of her coat. "I'm ready if you are."

"Let's go." Steve reached out and took her hand. He reopened the door. "Have a good night," He said to Shawn and Hazel.

"Bye!" Sara waved as she headed out the door.

Steve led her to his red sports car. He opened the passenger door for her and shut it once she was in. He walked around and got in the drivers side.

"This car is pretty cool." Sara said. "I don't know

anything about cars, what is it?"

"It's an Audi TT." Steve said proudly.

"Oh."

"I drove it off the lot a couple months ago."

"Still has that new car smell." Sara said.

"It sure does." Steve reversed out of the driveway. "Quite the light display you have."

Sara did not know how to respond. It wasn't a compliment to say thank you to. It was more of an observational statement.

"Yep," was all she could come up with.

Sara nervously fiddled with her purse. Steve boldly reached over and placed his hand on hers. He smiled at her quickly before putting his attention back to the road.

This guy's smooth.

Sara tried to relax. She sat back in the seat. She finally thought of a question, "How was Phoenix?"

"Sunny. The temperature got into the high sixties. I love being able to get away from these freezing short days. See the sun in December. I go to Phoenix about once a month keeping up a relationship with a customer there. Usually not for as long as this trip. I'll pop by for a day or two and move on as needed."

"Do you do a lot of traveling?"

Sara knew she could keep a conversation going if she could continue to think of questions.

"I fly to Vegas, L.A., San Francisco. I usually drive to Seattle. I pretty much rep the West Coast. The industry is booming. I have to make sure panels are always in stock. The sales teams know what they are doing. I have to wine and dine them, keep suppliers and store owners happy. I have a hefty expense account, and I basically get to enjoy the better things in life on the company's dime," Steve said with more than a hint of boastfulness.

"That sounds interesting."

Sara quickly thought of more questions. "I never thought to ask but do you have children?"

"I do. They live with their mother. Lindsey, who's twelve and Dillon that just turned eight. He's a real go getter, already excelling on his soccer team. Soccer skills run in the family."

Sara decided to take the bait, "You played soccer?"

"Yeah at U of O, for four years. We had a pretty great team when I was there. Went to the Independence Bowl, but couldn't bring it home," he said with regret.

"You're a Duck, huh?" Sara asked.

"Quack Quack. Cut me, I bleed green and yellow," Steve readily replied.

Sara knew nothing about soccer. Her mind was blank for a new line of questioning. She started to get self conscious of the silence as it dragged on. She decided to go with honesty.

"I'm sorry, I'm so nervous. I haven't really dated since before Hazel was born. That's a long time. I'm not sure exactly how to navigate this. "

"Oh, sweetheart. Don't worry about it. We get a couple drinks in us and the conversation will flow." He flashed Sara a dashing smile. Raising his hand he brushed his fingers in her hair. "Your hair is beautiful. I had to touch it. I hope you don't mind. It looked so soft and it is."

Sara was flattered. Having a man touch her hair felt nice. He seemed so confident. Sara didn't know what to think about it. She decided it must be the amount of entertaining he does for customers. Maybe he had been on the dating scene for a while.

He's right, a couple of cocktails will loosen us up.

"Thank you. I forgot to tell you how handsome you look tonight. It was really nice of you to pick me up. I didn't know if men still did that these days."

"It's no problem. Nothing better than driving a pretty woman."

"Flattery will get you everywhere." Sara joked.

"I'll keep it up then." Steve accelerated onto the highway. The car had some get up and go. Sara wondered if this was Steve's midlife crisis sports car. It was at least subtler than it could have been.

Sara smiled. This was nice. She was filled with electric anticipation for the evening. Scenarios flitted through her head. She wondered what his place looked like and if she would get to see it tonight?

"Do you live near the gym?" Sara asked remembering him shirtless in the sauna. It was nice to have already seen the merchandise and she approved.

"It's about a 10 minute drive. Did you go this week?"

"I sure did. But there were no more handsome men in the sauna. It was kind of a disappointment. You raised my expectations that maybe I'd get to sweat with hot men every day."

Steve laughed. She could tell he liked her stroking his ego. "Did you now? I'm sorry I couldn't be there for you." He took the next exit and entered one of the more high-end neighborhoods in town.

"I love this part of town." Sara said. "I take Hazel shopping at the quirky little boutiques over here."

After a few blocks Steve lucked into a parking spot on the street and parallel parked with ease.

"Ready?" He asked.

"I sure am." They both exited the car and met on the sidewalk. Steve took her hand and led the way to Alder Lounge.

Chapter Twelve

Adam was seated at the bar, sipping an eighteen year old Macallan scotch. He loved the smoky oak finish of this particular brand. Every glass was always superb. He was lucky they carried it. It was worth every penny and the only reason he would ever be at such a pretentious establishment. He wanted to at least be in the company of people tonight while he drank his favorite scotch. A loud bar might drown out the circling thoughts in his mind.

Adam's inner turmoil was relentless. The gnawing angst of loneliness and uncertainty swirling around the increasing amount of times Sara's smiling face popped into his head.

The bartender, a woman in her late forties with a black leather halter-top and torn to hell jeans eyed him. She was surprised at his drink choice. She had never seen a twenty something order such a top shelf scotch in the fifteen years she'd tended bar. This man was built and sexy as hell. She thought she might as well talk him up a little.

"Hope you knew what you were ordering. I can't pour it back in the bottle," she teased him. Adam just nodded. "You must come from money," she said with a lighthearted smirk. Her eyes knowingly roving him up and down.

Adam shrugged. He didn't care what she thought of his order and didn't want to have this conversation. He looked back down at his tumbler of amber liquid, swirled it around. The bartender trusted her people reading skills and knew this was the signal. If she wanted a good tip, this was a customer to leave be. She shoved off the bar and moved along.

Adam knew he needed to make connections in this town. He was beginning to succumb to a deep loneliness. He stared into his glass.

What am I going to do?

Adam's dream for a normal life was quickly deteriorating. His failed attempts at dating women the age he appeared to be were laughable. He was failing at human right now and he knew it.

Christmas was only a week away. Maybe he should just take that flight to Italy and spend it with his friends. He could tolerate Rebecca. He hated to admit it, but being alone for Christmas actually scared him. But the idea of showing up at the Villa put a bad taste in his mouth. Rebecca would know he was weak and lonely. It would be so easy to give up and go back to his vampire life. The holiday was shining a light on his loneliness in a way he was not prepared for.

This is brutal. If only Sara-

He shook his head at himself. He needed to stop. He at least had a plan now. He needed to focus on finding a woman in his age bracket.

I have eternity. I can handle one Christmas all alone, and hope by next year I've found someone.

He frowned into his glass of scotch before he picked it up and finished it off. The warm liquid traveled down and settled in his stomach, heating him up from the inside. He could feel it taking the edge off of his dread.

He heard joyful laughter over the buzz of a bar full of talking people.

Wait.

He knew that laugh. He had thought of that laugh every day for two weeks.

That's Sara!

His eyes opened wider and his face came to life. He did not want to be noticed, so he carefully scanned the tables and booths around the bar. He had to find the origin of that laugh.

He spotted her. She was glowing in an emerald green cocktail dress. Adam could not help but watch her. She laughed again which made Adam take notice to whom she was gifting such joy. Jealousy reared its ugly head.

She's on a date. Sara was on a date with a good-looking man in his forties.

That should be me. I'm forty in this fucking body. Damn Rebecca for this.

His jaw clenched down grinding his teeth. Defeated.

Good for her. I hope she's happy. He's one lucky man.

He had waited too long to turn back.

Their eyes met. Hers widened in recognition. She instantly smiled at him. It lightened his soul. She waved. Her date looked toward Adam.

Why did my body stand up? Goddamn it! I either have to sit back down or walk over.

Sara waved him over. He had no choice.

He's walking toward us!

Sara's heart began to pump double time in her chest.

This was the first time she had seen him upright.

Wow. Fuck.

Adam looked handsome as ever in faded jeans with a long sleeve flannel untucked over a form fitting black t-shirt. The flannel strained at the shoulders to contain their broadness. Strength emanated from his six foot four inch frame.

How genetically lucky can you get?!

Steve assessed the newcomer with a glance and dismissed him. Adam was too young to be a threat.

"It's so good to see you! Steve, this is Adam, the most fantastic Uber driver a girl could click for," Sara stood up and gushed a little too excitedly.

Steve stood up too and shook his hand. Adam's grasp a little tighter than he should have but he could not help himself. This guy was living the life he could never have.

"Uber driver, huh?" he said, on the edge of condescending. "How's that work?" Steve flexed his fingers after their hands released.

"Oh, I just pick up interesting women at all hours of the night."

He winked at Sara, never looking toward Steve as he replied. "Pretty great job and decent money," Adam replied.

Sara blushed. The wink and the eye contact from Adam made her face heat up. She had to remind herself that she was on a date with Steve. She forced herself to focus. She couldn't figure out what to say. Too many seconds had passed by as they stood in silence.

"Steve! Hey Steve!" A voice shouted over the noisy bar from the entrance where patrons waited for a table. Sara was relieved someone was rescuing her from this awkward situation. "What are you doing on this side of town?" The man's voice shouted over the crowd. It was an older couple. Steve went rigid.

The couple approached, having to sidestep between several cramped tables. Sara looked befuddled by the change in atmosphere. Steve seemed in a silent panic. Sara could feel the tension radiate from his body. He looked trapped. Sara couldn't figure out why.

Adam understood right away. Steve had the stench of guilt and flop sweat emanating from his pours. Steve was obviously not supposed to be on a date. The bastard.

The couple arrived at the table, which had two place settings not three. Steve scrambled to switch where he was standing with Adam. Adam would not budge.

There were too many moments of awkwardness for Sara. She watched as Steve tried to swap places with Adam. She decided introducing herself was in order since Steve had obviously forgotten proper etiquette. "Hi. I'm Sara."

She smiled at them, but it faltered. She noticed the couple noticing the romantic setting, her obvious "I'm on a date" outfit. That Steve was standing up in front of the only other chair.

The gray haired couple had wide eyes on Steve.

The man cleared his throat, "Hi Sara, Steve here is our son-in-law." He looked toward Sara, who now had her full deducting capability and her mouth wide open.

Adam, always quick to take full advantage of opportunity had his wallet out handing a passing waitress a fifty. "That's for the bartender."

He turned back to the unfolding scene, "I'm Adam, one fantastic Uber driver. That I'm guessing Sara here is in need of right now." He grabbed her jacket and purse off her chair, and her hand as she sputtered nonsense about being appalled. They left Steve behind to deal with his own mess. Adam led Sara out of the bar and into the night.

Chapter Thirteen

Once on the sidewalk outside the bar, Adam stopped and spun Sara around to face him. He gently put her jacket on her like she was a child. She passively allowed him. He buttoned her up patiently. Adam looked at her and waited.

She stood there thinking through it all, not looking up yet.

That cheating son of a bitch. His poor wife.

God damn it...

Wait a minute. I'm standing on a sidewalk with this boy who makes my knees weak.

Oh my goodness.

Hmm...

Should I dare...

"Fuck it," she said under her breath making Adam smile. She looked up into his eyes and said, "Wanna get a drink before you drive me home?"

"Yes, more than anything." He replied.

He grabbed her hand and they walked a block in silence to the next bar.

"How long have you been dating good ole Steve?" Adam asked once their drinks were in front of them. They were tucked away in a dark corner at a tiny table for two.

"It was our first date. Thankfully."

Adam was relieved. She couldn't have had any feelings for that dirtbag and he wouldn't be consoling her tonight.

"Thank you for the rescue. I hope I'm not keeping you from any plans. It was an impulse to ask you for a drink. You're so nice you couldn't turn me down after that happened." She started to doubt herself and thought she'd better give him an out. Was she keeping him from a night out with friends or a date? "Oh no, were you waiting for your girlfriend? I can't believe I just assumed you could come here and have time to sit with me. You're so sweet. How could you turn me down? I'm sorry."

"Before you work yourself up." Adam held his hand up. "I was at the bar alone and was waiting on no one. And now you know I'm a dork and a loner. You can bow out gracefully yourself if you want."

Sara giggled, "Me bow out! Ha! I'm thirty-nine and just found out the first man to ask me on a date in well over a decade has a wife. You're young and gorgeous. I wouldn't care if you were Jack the Ripper right now." She laughed. Adam had an odd look in his eye she couldn't read. She coughed to cover up the awkward moment and drank a big swallow of her gin and tonic.

Adam took a long swallow of his scotch. His eyes were so intense, the maturity of them at odds with his young face. His eyes spoke of a life of experience but his face was lineless.

"I love the dress. New?" He gave her an appraising look.

She laughed and decided to be her honest self, "I bought it because it was the color of your eyes." She held her breath for his response to her telling remark. A smile began in his eyes and continued until all his sparkling straight white teeth were showing. His smile was dazzling. She couldn't help but return it.

They both grabbed their drinks and took a sip.

What is happening? She thought. *This is unbelievable. Maybe a one-night stand with an older woman wasn't out of the question. Interesting.*

She didn't know for how long she could pretend that a man like this would really want her for anything other than sex.

Who am I kidding? I want him for the sex.

Fuck it girl, go for it!

She decided to take full advantage of the situation and enjoy herself.

"Can I tell you something?" She asked.

"I am all ears."

"You remember the first Uber ride?"

"Of course. You could sing every word of Lump, you got my jokes and made even funnier ones," he replied.

Sara smiled, "Yes, but aside from all that, it sparked something inside me that spurned on a much needed change in my life. I didn't see much of a romantic future for myself. I've hit an age where the men in my dating pool are either a decade older than me, or if my age, are otherwise undesirable. But you... you are so adorable." He gave her a funny look.

"Adorable?" He said it with a little sneer.

Laughing, Sara continued, "Yes adorable! You are handsome, gorgeous and adorable."

She paused and took a fortifying sip while motioning to the waitress for the next round. "So I felt a spark of change when I got home that day. I was ready for something different. I started taking better care of myself instead of putting myself last. I got my hair done."

Sara flipped her hair, showing it off. Adam eyed her locks appreciatively.

"I requested that second Uber ride. I looked at that app for ten minutes and finally just went for it. I felt brave and alive." She took a breath, looking into his jewel green eyes. "I bought new clothes, including this tribute to your eyes dress. I let the Universe know I was ready and available. Then I got asked out on that date although it was a disaster, getting asked out felt amazing! I've been feeling really good and somehow it all came about because of you."

Adam stared at her quietly for a moment. He opened his mouth to respond.

Sara held up her hand. "Don't say anything yet. I'm thirty-nine. I'm not a silly girl. I can see you. You're young and handsome. Too young and too handsome." She sighed, "...but you're fun and vibrant and..." She shrugged, "Whatever. I want to have fun. Will you have *fun* with me tonight?"

"Yes, Sara," he said, his green eyes sparkling in the overhead light.

"Good! Glad we had this conversation." She smiled and folded her hands in her lap.

"Me too." His gaze was direct, acknowledging his understanding of her invitation. "Do you want to order food? I think the plate you left behind was full."

"Oh, it was! I'm totally starving. How about you?"

"I ate dinner already, but tonight's on me. You've had quite the evening. Order whatever you'd like." He declared.

"Far be it from me to get in the way of chivalry. Let me

have a look at this menu." She was giddy.

He watched her devour a burger and a sizeable side of tater tots with ranch. He was impressed and a little jealous. Sara seemed so light hearted and happy. She talked eagerly about her daughter and her best friend Shawn. She told him all about going out with Shawn and receiving her very first dick pic.

"Do you wanna see it?" She laughed and wiggled her eyebrows suggestively.

"Hell yeah, I want to see it," Adam replied which made her almost fall off her chair.

Their banter was fun and invigorating. She laughed a lot and made lots of jokes. Just sitting here at a table with her made him feel lighter. He felt almost human again. He could tell she was nervous. She could not hold his eye contact long. He wondered what she was thinking.

He knew what he looked like. Rebecca had picked him for a reason. She wanted a trophy mate and made sure she got one. She wanted to be superior to all the others and be the most beautiful couple in her realm. And they were. Heads turned when they entered rooms. It was flattering at first to have such a powerful woman choose him and give him immortality. He thought himself in love with her.

He knew Sara wanted him for his face and body right now. That was fine. He wanted her for how she made him feel. He wanted to prolong this connection, to feel normal for as long as he could. He had been so lonely for so long. She made him laugh and she was such a loving person.

He watched her closely, her blue eyes vibrant as she took the last sip of her cocktail. Her low cut green dress accented her creamy pale skin and full breasts. He saw her shiver. Goosebumps ran down her arm. He could feel the electric excitement pulsing off her body. It was contagious. He could not help but respond to her energy. She brought him to life and he loved it.

Sara's body would not stop shivering. She was so full of butterflies. The dinner was drawing to an end. She had practically spelled out she was game for sex. He'd accepted her invitation. She was getting laid tonight by this hot young man. She could not believe it! Shawn and Hazel were going to die when they found out.

She had finished her entrée and took the last sip of her drink.

I don't think I'm drunk enough for this. This man has to be sleeping with twenty-something models. What am I doing?

"I'm hoping you don't live in an apartment with five other frat guys. My daughter is home tonight." Sara said nervously.

He laughed and grabbed her hand he had seen shaking. "Relax. I live alone in a boring little house."

"I'm sorry. I'm just so nervous, excited, scared. Did I say excited? Ugh and I'm a dork." She rolled her eyes at herself.

Adam could hear her heart racing. He tried to ignore it.

"I should get one more drink. I need to forget who I am." She glanced toward her empty glass.

"Nope. I'd rather be sure of your consent. Otherwise I'll be tucking you in at your home tonight. Your daughter might wonder why a stranger is reading you a bedtime story."

Sara smiled, "I'm sorry. I just want to not be me for the

night. I want to forget I'm thirty-nine."

"Don't worry. I can make you forget. May I kiss you Sara?" His voice was deep and mesmerizing. He pulled her hand toward him and placed her palm on his chest.

"Yes," she breathed.

This was the moment she had imagined a hundred times. She couldn't believe this night could actually be happening. His hand reached up and tucked a strand of hair back behind her ear. He traced his fingers down her jaw and gently tipped her face up to meet his kiss.

Oh my god, this....

All thoughts left her head. His lips were gentle but firm and his hand went from her chin to slide back through her hair. Her hair was thick and soft. They were both starving for this connection. Sara's heart was pounding in her chest. She felt electrified by his lips. His tongue swept into her mouth and she met it with her own. Her body responded with sparks of passion she hadn't known were so deep within her.

He pulled away first. His eyes bright and intense with need, "You ready to go?"

"Umm, yes!" She said in a breathless voice. Her hand was still in his against his chest. Adam put her hand back on the table. He took out his wallet and threw cash down. He stood up and offered her his hand. Sara grabbed it and they started for the door.

Adam opened up the passenger side door and with grand flare welcomed Sara to the front seat.

"My lady, sit beside me? Unless you just prefer the backseat." He winked and smiled at her as she pretended to contemplate if she really wanted to sit beside him.

Adam watched Sara sparkle in the light of the street lamp. Her eyes shined up at him. She was vibrant and full of joy. Little jokes made her giggle. She didn't put on a show or fake who she was. She was Sara and she was lovely. She stepped past him and entered the passenger seat.

"This is nice." She said. "I think I like it up here."

"I like it, too," Adam said looking into her eyes before shutting the door. He walked around the car with a spring in his step. He hadn't felt this alive in sixteen years.

I've got to rock her world tonight. I will exceed expectations. I got this!

Determined, he jumped into the driver seat and turned on his Durango. Adam deftly maneuvered his vehicle out of the cramped parking lot. A group of drunk girls appeared and stumbled out from between two large SUV's. Adam dodged them expertly, narrowly avoiding another car reversing without looking.

"You've got the skills to pay the bills," Sara said, relieved.

Adam was always surprised when she made pop culture references to his own generation. She had no idea that he listened to that Beastie Boys album in high school just like she did. He took her hand and said, "They call me Ad-Rock." Sara giggled with surprise. He loved calling her on her old references.

"I forgot about your retro obsession. I love it! Helps me forget that you're too young for me."

Sadness clouded his emerald eyes. He looked away from her.

I'm not too young for you!

He knew she could never know what he was and she would never see him for anything but a one-night stand adventure. A fantasy. Nothing tangible. Nothing she could build a life on.

Sara squeezed his hand. "I'm going to shut up now."

Adam knew he had to get ahold of himself and bring things back on track. He turned to glance at her, the sadness gone. He took the next curve at a racer's pace. He smirked a rascal smile and winked at her. He took his hand from hers and softly ran it into her hair. As soft as a feather, he touched the skin on the back of her neck, making her shiver.

They rode on in a sexually charged silence.

"We're almost there." Adam said.

"Thank god!" She exclaimed. He smiled.

Turning onto a quiet street Adam pulled into his driveway and continued into his garage. He turned the car off and clicked the garage door closed.

Chapter Fourteen

Sara's stomach flipped upside down as the door slowly closed behind them. He turned off his car. She was now locked into a space with a man she didn't really know, in his home.

She started to question her choices and consider the safety of what she was doing. It had seemed like an amazing idea, but now she needed to reconfirm her safety.

"Do you mind taking a quick pic with me for my daughter and Shawn. I want her to know where I am. I also want to brag to Shawn. He'll be a jealous bitch and I love that. "

Okay. If he's cool with this evidence being sent out, I can relax again.

"Of course."

Relieved by his willingness, Sara got her IPhone out of her purse and swiped to camera. She leaned in toward Adam and he put his arm around her pulling her in tight. Sara raised an eyebrow and smiled a knowing smile into the camera. Adam grinned. Click.

"Bear with me. I have to make two separate captions: one for my teen daughter and one for my best friend."

"What about all your followers on IG?" Adam joked

referencing the bad date he had told her about when they first met.

She stuck her tongue out at him and laughed. Adam couldn't help but be curious of what she would caption. He blatantly watched to find out. Under the picture to be sent to her daughter, *"I don't know when I'll be home. Be good. You have to wait to find out why my night is ending up this way… and I didn't even wear cheetah print…"* Adam quizzically looked at Sara for an explanation. Sara tapped send.

"It's a bit of an inside joke." Sara coughed and was too embarrassed to explain the cougar reference. She didn't want to bring up age again this evening.

She texted the picture to Shawn and captioned, *"Now who's living life to the fullest, bitch? Don't call me too early tomorrow."* Adam's arm was still around her shoulders and he was lightly tracing his fingers along the neckline of her dress. Sara tapped send and took a deep breath. She returned her cellphone to her purse. It chimed one alert after another. They both laughed at the quick responses from Hazel and Shawn. Sara made no attempt to check what they had to say.

"Ready?" Adam said.

"Yes." They both exited the SUV.

Sara looked around the garage. It was surprisingly tidy for a garage.

So he's neat. That's good.

She followed him through the door. It connected to the kitchen, which was also clean and obviously not used much.

"You must eat out a lot?" She said taking in the details.

"Every meal." He smirked at his own inside joke.

"How do you stay in such good shape if you eat that much fast food?"

"I work out." He said. "Can you stay here while I make sure there is nothing embarrassing out anywhere? I wasn't expecting to bring someone back here tonight."

"Of course." Sara said.

"Can you mix up a couple drinks? Booze is in the cabinet and there's ice in the freezer." Adam requested.

"Sure."

Adam walked out of the kitchen and Sara went to work on the drinks. She also did a little snooping on the side. The first cabinet she opened was completely empty.

How weird.

Second cabinet had an array of top shelf liquor.

For a twenty-four year old he has excellent taste. Must have come from a wealthy family.

She grabbed Russian vodka and continued her search for glasses. She opened three more cabinets to find them but noticed not a single cabinet held any plates or bowls.

That's strange.

"Bachelor life is weird." She mumbled.

Adam hurriedly threw his underwear and dirty clothes into the hamper in his bathroom. He sucked down the last drop from a cold blood donor bag. Drinking it cold was unappealing but would satiate him nonetheless. He didn't want to think about how Sara's blood would taste while having sex with her tonight. He didn't need that temptation. He stashed the spent bag at the bottom of the hamper.

Adam rinsed out his mouth at the sink and brushed his teeth quickly. He didn't want to have blood breath either. He spit and looked into the mirror. He felt satisfied for now. The anticipation for what was to come made him fidgety. He looked into his eyes in the mirror.

You got this. Get back out there and be charming. Knock her socks off. He nodded at himself in the mirror.

Adam pushed away from the sink and headed back to the kitchen.

Sara was waiting, vodka on the rocks in hand, when Adam entered the kitchen.

"Your cupboards are pretty sparse." She stated while handing him one of the drinks. Already her brain contemplating ways to fix his empty cupboard problem, always a giver, Sara could not help it.

"You want to put on an old movie?" Adam asked. They were both getting awkward. They obviously needed a distraction to take the pressure off.

He led her into the living room. Sara glanced around, taking in the new room. It was masculine in décor. Another unexpected neat room with sparse yet well appointed furnishings.

Adam opened a sliding door shelving unit to display an impressive Blu-ray collection. His arm around her shoulder, they scanned the titles. A lot of today's blockbusters but a large selection of 80's and 90's favorites and some obscure films Sara had grown up with. Sara's eyes stopped at Die Hard and her hand automatically grabbed it.

"Die Hard for sure!"

Adam's eyes lit up. "Yes, most definitely! Best Christmas movie ever!"

"I always say that!" She exclaimed putting her hand up for a high five.

Delighted, he hadn't high fived anyone in so long he

couldn't remember. Their hands clapped together and they shared big smiles. Adam turned on his TV and loaded the movie. Sara made herself comfortable on the sofa and took a sip of her drink. She sat it down on the end table. Full of nervous energy, she felt like a teenager again.

Are we going to make out on the couch while watching a movie?!! Sara was all smiles, she almost giggled.

Adam turned around to see her ear-to-ear grin.

"That smile of yours..." He said struck speechless. His mouth responded in kind with a smile that lit up his green eyes. His straight white teeth were perfectly framed by full lips. He could not help himself. He needed her now. He sat his drink down on the TV stand.

Adam's smile turned into a knowing grin. His eyes intense, sparking green flames of passionate promises. He walked straight to her and knelt down in one fluid motion between her knees.

Sara let out a surprised gasp of anticipation. Her breath quickened. At his height he was eye to eye with her. Adam took her face in his hands not breaking eye contact until the last moment. Finally his lips melted into hers.

Sara was taken aback for a moment at the rapid escalation to the evening but quickly got on board and responded with unbridled passion of her own. Her arms wrapped around his broad shoulders. She ran her fingers along the skin on the back of his neck and up into his soft hair.

Adam's strong hands held her face. He slanted his mouth over hers to deepen the kiss and taste her fully. She tasted of vodka and honey. He couldn't get enough. Sara's fingers running through his hair felt tender and loving. He pulled back to shallow the kiss and ended it with soft kisses along her lower lip drawing it into his mouth gently. Adam turned her head to the side and trailed kisses along the length of her neck, soft and deliberately slow. Sara's head fell back and she let out a sweet little moan.

She ran her hands to the sides of his face and lifted it, bringing his eyes back to look into hers. She kissed him this time with the pent up passion of an unsatisfied woman. She devoured him.

Sara wanted this man more than she'd ever desired a man before. The fire in her veins pulsed through her heart erratically. His kiss was perfect. His tongue suckled at her own following her lead this time. Fingers grazed her nipples over her dress that sent a ripple of electricity down to the pit of her belly.

Sara let her hand move from the sides of his face down his chest. It was hard and defined. She shivered as she felt his abs through his shirt. She gathered up his t-shirt at the bottom in her fingers and put her hands on his tight flat belly. His skin was hot. She made a sexy sound in the back of her throat as their kiss continued. Adam's hand came up to hold her chin as he deepened the kiss.

Sara explored the ripples of his muscles as she ran her hand back up his chest where she teased his nipples. She ended the deep kiss reluctantly. Kissing his lips several times before she looked back into his eyes. Her breathing was shallow and fast, her arousal beyond anything she'd ever experienced before. She could barely think a full thought.

This is exactly what she'd been fantasizing about for weeks. His strong hand held her chin as they searched each other's eyes.

"Wow." Sara breathed. "Fuck Die Hard."

Adam smirked, "I mean I love me some Bruce Willis

but I'm going to enjoy this so much more." He grabbed the remote from the side table and clicked off the TV.

"Yippee-Ki-Yay, Motherfucker!" Sara exclaimed making Adam laugh.

He stood up and in one graceful move picked her up on his way to standing. He held her with her feet off the ground against his body. She wrapped her arms around his neck. Adam leaned forward to kiss her. He held her up so they were lip to lip. Sara, too curious to continue, ended the kiss and leaned back to look him in the eyes. He didn't seem to be straining to support her weight. She quizzically looked down toward her dangling feet and back at his eyes.

Adam realized he probably shouldn't have shown her this much of his strength. Sara made him forget to pretend to be human. Being so strongly built, he figured she would accept his response of, "I power lift."

Sara smiled. Impressed.

"I love that." She breathed.

He swung her up into his arms with ease. Sara put her ear to his rock hard chest and looked up at his chiseled jaw. He looked down into her adoring eyes and felt the equivalent of his knees going weak, as much as a vampire can go weak. The trust and pureness of adoration in her gaze was humbling. Her sparkling blue eyes enchanted him.

"Would you like to see my bedroom?" Adam asked.

"Why, yes. Yes I would." She giggled. "Oh wait, grab my purse. I bring my own condoms. I have a favorite brand."

Adam raised his eyebrow in question. "A favorite brand, huh?"

He winked at her. He knew she was too smart of a

woman to be careless with her health. She didn't have anything to worry about but she didn't know that. He grabbed her little bag and stopped.

Curious he asked, "What might I ask is this favorite brand?"

"You can't get them at any store. I have to order them special. But once you try it you can't go back to the cheap ones."

"Really? You are an intriguing woman, Sara," Adam said, a bemused look on his face. She put one in his hand.

"Now quit your lollygagging and let's go see that bedroom," Sara demanded jokingly.

"Alrighty then." Adam mimicked Ace Ventura. Sara burst out laughing. She'd seen it in his movie collection and knew he was really referencing a movie from 1994.

How amazing it felt to Adam to carry this woman in his arms to bed while they both laughed. He was walking on air. So close to human. Happy.

He put her down once he entered his bedroom. She looked around satisfying the snoop in her. Another clean room. The bed was actually made. She put her purse down on the chest of drawers.

With a determined glint in her eye she turned back to him and pushed his flannel up and over his broad shoulders removing it. In response his hands went for her dress straps.

Sara swatted his hands away, "Not yet. Let me play first."

His eyebrows went up and she smiled devilishly. She lifted his t-shirt slowly revealing abs that made her sigh loudly.

Adam smiled down at her. Looking like his 24 year old self had its perks. He helped her take off his t-shirt since she wasn't tall enough to lift it over his head easily. Sara ran her fingers slowly along the planes and curves of his defined body. Her fingers trembled with nervous energy.

Sara leaned forward, kissed his chest and teasingly licked around his nipple until she took it into her mouth. He sucked in his breath. She nipped at his skin and kissed a trail to his waist. Sara ran her fingers inside the waistband of his jeans. Goosebumps raised on his flat toned belly. The V shaped muscle leading down into his jeans flexed as she unbuttoned his pants. Sara licked her lips and shivered in anticipation for what was at the end of it.

She put her hands inside his boxers to feel his swollen dick. He was hard and big. Sara was delighted. Her body was on fire for him. She was relishing every moment. She pushed his pants down to get a look at him. The V taper of his abs ended in the most beautiful cock she had ever seen. Stout and long, she couldn't wait to feel it enter her. But first she wanted to spend some time enjoying this man.

Sara looked up into his glittering jewel green eyes. His expression animalistic and in the sexiest move she'd ever made she dropped to her knees without breaking eye contact. Adam's eyes ignited.

Sara gently cupped his balls with one hand and held the base of his cock with the other. She began to lick his shaft, wetting his cock to easily move her hand and mouth in unison. She took him into her mouth and suckled, moving her tongue in rhythm with her hand and mouth. Twirling her tongue around the tip then taking him deep again and again. He was moaning. His breath hitching.

"Fuck yeah." His voice hoarse. "Oh Sara. Yes.... Shit." Adam's hips jerked and he swayed on his feet, "Unless you want me to come in your mouth I can't take much more."

She slowly removed his dick from her lips. Teasingly kissed his erection and gently released him. Adam grabbed her off the ground like she weighed nothing. He was beyond trying to regulate his strength. She bounced when her body hit the bed. She giggled. She had made him urgent with need. It was incredible. Her body was singing with anticipation.

Adam stood at the edge of the bed, breathing heavily. He kicked off his pants and shoes. He gently grabbed her by the ankle and removed one shoe then the other. Her legs were smooth and bare. He ran his hands up her calves. She shivered. He followed, moving up her long legs and climbed onto the bed. He ran his fingers teasingly around the edge of her panties.

"These better be wet." He said. She bit her lip at his hot words, her breathing loud and quick.

He pulled her panties down her legs. They were black and lacy. A new pair she had gotten recently in hopes of getting lucky. She never expected to get this lucky.

"You are making me burn." Sara almost growled.

He smiled at her and bent down to kiss the side of her knee. Her body was vibrating with excitement. He kissed and lightly licked at the underside of her knee. She made uncontrollable feminine sounds. He put her leg back down and traced his fingers back up to her pussy, kissing her legs as he traveled upwards. He spread her legs farther and settled himself between her thighs. Adam lifted her dress to see her. He was rock hard at the thought of tasting her.

Adam lowered his head to kiss and stroke her clit with his tongue. He suckled it while gently stroking her with his fingers.

"I think I'm going to come already!!" Sara panted, the

hot tight knot deep in her belly building pressure she knew was about to shatter.

Adam raised his head slightly and urgently whispered, "Come in my mouth."

Those words were all it took. She was pulsing into his suckling lips. She screamed, digging her nails into his shoulders bucking herself deeper into his mouth. The waves subsided and her hips relaxed.

"Wow." Sara breathed.

Adam looked up at her with eyes like hot green coals. "I'm not finished with you yet."

"I hope not, honey. I need that dick." She said with a smile.

"I'm dying to fuck you, but let's make this last."

He climbed up her body like a stalking lion. The length of his body on top of hers. She opened her mouth to accept his passionate kiss. She could taste herself on his lips and her body began to ache with need. The kiss was hot and reckless.

He tore his mouth away and kissed down her neck pulling the straps of her dress off her shoulders. He pressed hot wet kisses down her chest, slowly pulling her straps farther down to reveal her breasts. He took an erect nipple into his hot mouth. His mouth scorched her skin. She melted into the mattress.

"Oh, Adam. Yes!" She grabbed his head putting her fingers through his soft hair. He circled her nipple with his tongue before he sucked it deep and hard. He kissed his way to her other nipple giving it the same attention.

"How much do you love this dress?" He asked.

Sara read his mind. "I love it, but fuck it."

Adam ripped it to shreds and threw the pieces on the floor. His naked body came down on top of hers. He held her face and kissed her lips as his cock found it's way to the dripping wet heat between her legs. His solid masculine body, skin to skin with hers was heaven for Sara. He held his body weight off of her with one hand and used the other to hold her to him while he glided in his throbbing cock.

"Fuck! Yes!" Sara exclaimed. She felt his thick dick enter her, passing her g spot, completely filling her, stretching her to fullness.

Adam grunted in male satisfaction and withdrew to begin the ritual as old as time.

"Sara, Oh Sara." He chanted.

She was crazed with pleasure. She grasped at his ass. He slowly teased her and pulled out to slowly reenter. It was exquisite. She could feel his entire shaft moving within her, his thick head entered her pussy over and over. Sara reveled in it. His thrusts pounded against her clit at that perfect angle, stoking the fire of her release. Her belly tightened ready to come again.

"I'm going to come! Oh my god!" Sara yelled.

"Come on my dick, baby." Adam's strained voice deep and sexy.

Time stopped. Sara's body arched in an infinite moment of ecstasy.

She exploded into her climax yelling, "Adam Fuck Holy Fuck!"

Watching her come drove him wild. He could feel every throbbing pulse of her orgasm on his cock. It did not take much more before his body tightened above her and he shouted his release. His body trembling with shockwaves of pleasure pulsating through him.

Adam collapsed on top of her trying to catch his breath.

"Adam." Sara said.

He kissed her to hush and settled beside her. They sighed in unison both relaxed back on their pillows.

Sara's smile was ear to ear. This turned out perfect. She was the Cheshire Cat right now.

Adam glanced at her and caught the smile.

"The kind of "fun" evening you were hoping for?" He asked.

"You have no idea." She looked up at the mounted TV across the room above his dresser. "Is it weird that I still want to watch Die Hard?"

Adam looked at her, his expression changing from surprise at her request to Goddess worship of her for making it.

Chapter Fifteen

Sara fell asleep ten minutes into Die Hard. Adam watched her sleep in the glow of the TV. He knew she considered this a one-night stand. He knew she took full advantage of tonight with such abandon, only because she felt no pressure that there could ever be more. He was just a boy to her.

Adam pushed a lock of hair behind her ear. This had honestly been the best night of his life. The memory of her on her knees in front of him made him shiver.

Rebecca wouldn't get on her knees for anyone.

He hated thinking of her. She was his maker. He had spent fifteen years with her. At the time, he thought that was all life would be for him. Empty. Shallow. Blood and sex.

Adam pulled Sara closer to him. She instinctively snuggled into him and made a noise in her sleep. She was a ray of pure warmth. Adam was not ready to let go of her. He had felt more human in the times spent with her than he had in fifteen years.

After his parent's death, Adam actually preferred that he didn't feel human. It was much easier that way. To be separate from human feelings. To live a life above the sea of humanity. Vampires had cultivated quite the culture among themselves. They knew they held dominion in this world. They held themselves in very high esteem, being above humans in every way. Vampires new to the life were given what you could describe as an appointed social worker, to guide the newcomer through the changes, cravings and new powers that would develop.

The older Vampires hadn't been so lucky. They had lived through their early years with an unquenchable bloodthirst that led to years of slaughter. Their inner human squelched with killing. A vampire in those days couldn't undo the death and carnage they had wrought, and the loss of their humanity was the cost.

Today, the mental health of new vampires was taken into consideration. They were walked through the new life. Controlled. They were taught to live a life without killing humans, freeing them of the mental anguish suffered by the older generations.

Mental health was a big deal in today's Vampire culture. A Vampire could wreak a lot of havoc, bring attention to The Collective, if they were to go off the handle. Evidence was too easy to leave behind in today's world. One Vampire going into a rage could bring unwanted attention to all, so the Elders now considered mental health of the utmost importance.

Adam's case manager, Caelum, had been with him every step of the way for the first five years after his transformation. He made sure Adam never went thirsty. A new vampire needed to always be satisfied or the temptation would easily get the better of them. That was not an option in the modern world. The toll of murder on a new Vampire's mind was too much and the implications on their behavior down the road were predictable. Depression and anger turned into acts of violence and more murder. Adam was thankful that he had been turned in this time and not a hundred years ago. He didn't need memories like that.

The kind of memories that he knew had twisted Rebecca's mind. Rebecca was turned in the early 1700s. She was well respected among the Elders. The vampires that could not adjust to the 21st century, ones that had become more monster than human, had been eliminated. Only a handful of the untamed had survived staying hidden from the Elders. Everyone else had to assimilate and adapt to the new era. They had to play a better part in society. Which Rebecca could do. If an Elder couldn't stop killing they had to become smarter. Vampires did not bite to kill any longer. The only times they used their teeth to drain blood was during sex or with a vetted *Volunteer*. Those still bent on the kill and drain learned to use blades to make each death look like a human crime or suicide.

Adam did not realize the extent of Rebecca's loss of humanity for many years. She had hidden it well. He thought her to be as civilized as himself. He knew she had spent hundreds of years killing, but only thought it was because that was the times she had lived in. It was years later that he found out she was still satisfying her thirst for human blood with murder. He could not stomach it. She cried to him that he did not understand, that things were different when she was turned. She could not change. She could not stop the need. She raged against him.

"Who do you think you are? Judging me! You know nothing! Nothing!! Caelum held your hand like a fucking toddler for five years! I was thrown into the world thirsty, blood lusting, every sense heightened. My maker satisfied me the only way I could be satisfied. Fuck you, Adam!"

He remembered her rage at him. She twisted the

tables and he was the intolerant one that should love her no matter what. Because of her indoctrination into this life, she laid no blame at her own feet.

Adam tried. He wasn't human anymore and lived among many Elders he called friends. They were all he had, and had accepted him immediately. They may have lived a millennia but within an instant he was part of their extended family. How could he judge them? They had lived a completely different life for hundreds of years. They were evolving and that was commendable.

Sara began to lightly snore. Adam smiled. He was going to be awake the rest of the night. He usually stayed available to drive riders around. He stared down at her contented to stay right there for a while.

This woman had everything he needed to feel whole again. He could imagine them living just like his parents had lived. They were happy and full of life. They completed each other. He had taken for granted while he was human that he would turn out just like them. He always knew he'd find just the right girl, settle down, love a great woman, and become a great dad.

Will you save me, Sara?

Chapter Sixteen

Not my bed! Sara woke up startled.

The night's events flashed in her mind. She smiled and stretched like a well fed cat, still sporting that Cheshire grin. Adam was not in the room. She wondered what time it was. Her phone was in her purse on the dresser. She sat up naked, remembering what had happened to her dress.

Shit! What the hell am I supposed to wear home?

Sara got out of bed and looked around for her panties, locating them on the floor next to a piece of her beautiful green dress. She felt him before she saw him. She finished pulling up her panties and turned around to see him leaning on the doorframe.

He was smiling with a to-go coffee in his hand held out to her. She returned his grin and walked over to grab it.

"Good timing. Thank you!" Taking a sip she knew he remembered her order from Sweet Beans. Her grin deepened. "I have a little wardrobe dilemma."

"Yes you do." Adam replied. He watched her sip her coffee in only her panties. His smile deepened. "I'm not really sure I want to help you solve it," he said like the charmer he was. His eyes roved over her slowly.

"Since it's all your fault, you must."

"I distinctly remember hearing you say, fuck it.... In

more ways than one." He smiled at his joke and Sara giggled.

"I think there's probably a rule against Ubering half naked women."

"Help yourself to anything in my closet." He replied.

"I'm guessing I'm not lucky enough for you to cross-dress on the weekends?" Sara winked at him. "Old girlfriend left her crap here?"

"It's really hard to find a flattering dress in my size. I had to give up the dream." Adam ignored the second question.

"Awww," Sara replied with a fake sad face.

Sara couldn't help but happily skip to the closest. Great sex will do that to you. She opened the door to find well-organized clothing and shoes. She inhaled the scent of clean clothes and Adam. She took a long drag off her coffee, enjoying the sensory overload of this perfect morning. She saw a long sleeve light blue plaid flannel. She put her coffee down and slipped it on. The sleeves hung past her hands. She held the too long sleeved arms out in front of herself. She laughed at the thought of walking through her front door dressed like this.

Adam walked by his dresser picking up one of her condoms, just in case, and stepped up behind her. He put his hands on her shoulders. Sara instinctively leaned back against his strong chest. He nuzzled his face into her neck. He reveled in the humanness of this morning. He couldn't help himself but try to prolong the contact. He heard her sigh.

She looked adorable in his big flannel shirt. He wanted her again. The moment he saw her naked looking for her panties on the floor amongst the torn remnants of her dress he was rock hard. Spending the night with her had been a pleasure beyond any experience he'd had with a woman. There was warmth growing in his chest. A feeling of home attached to this woman.

He had been afraid she would wake up and want to leave sometime in the night. Thankful she hadn't. He hoped to show her a good time this morning.

Adam lightly ran an arm around her and glided his hand over a nipple. She shivered in response to his light touch. He cupped her breast in his head, feeling her nipple harden beneath it.

Sara was surprised. This young man was going above and beyond. She was taken aback yet game for enjoying more, she spun around in his arms.

She met his sensual questioning gaze with eyes that said, yes.

Sara took a deep breath and said, "Kind of wish I would have had time to brush my teeth." Adam smirked and shook his head in response. He grabbed her face in his hands. The descent of his lips was exquisite anticipation. The electric current she felt in her body almost buckled her knees.

His lips crushed hers and devoured her. She tasted like a delicious hazelnut latte. Sara's knees could not take anymore and gave way. Before she could fall, Adam grabbed her up into the air and splayed her legs around his waist.

"God, your strong!" She breathed.

He pulled up her shirt and grabbed her panties between his fingers.

Sara heard the rip, realized what he had done and started laughing. "You are really hard on a lady's clothes!"

"Sorry, I blame you for driving me to it."

Their eyes locked and time stood still. Sara's head tilted to the right as she studied his eyes. With one hand he easily held her with her legs wrapped around him. He unbuttoned his jeans and released his erection. Sara held on while he used both hands to secure the condom he knew she required. Sara was impressed with the fact she did not have to say anything. She felt his dick rub against her bottom and trembled in expectation.

"Oh god! Yes." She could not believe she was living in this fantasy. Her belly tightened with desire for his entrance.

Adam lifted her and settled her deliciously, slowly onto his thick cock. Sara's head fell back as she savored every moment. When he filled her completely she wrapped her arms around his neck. She hugged him. She never wanted to let him go. Sara knew this would be a sexual encounter never to be topped. She would never forget this and would be forever grateful to Adam. She hugged him harder. Her heart was weighted in her chest, anchoring her to this man right now.

Can he feel this? She wondered but dismissed herself thinking, *of course he couldn't. How could he possibly? Don't overthink just enjoy yourself.*

Adam looked down at Sara hugging him with an expression he interpreted as bliss on her face. The hug was so genuine. What they were doing was intimate but this hug was true human intimacy. He put both of his arms around her and squeezed in return. They stayed like this breathing in unison. His chest was heavy and hot. Adam saw in his mind a vision of golden light cords of his soul connected to her heart. He saw their souls entwined. His heart pumped deep and hard as if it pumped for them both.

The intensity of this new vampire emotion overwhelmed him. Was this what it felt to connect to your lifemate? He knew without a doubt it was. He knew at that moment he had to try to win her. He did not know if she could fall in love with him, but he had to give it everything he had. This woman was all he wanted in life.

He began to withdraw from her barely letting himself exit her before slowly entering her again. She moaned deep in her throat. There was nothing more decadent than this. He walked while still inside her to the nearest bare wall. Sara felt the wall at her back and she leaned against it. She unbuttoned his shirt, revealing a t-shirt underneath. Disappointed, she wanted nothing between them.

"Take it off!" She ordered while she spread her own shirt revealing her lovely breasts. Adam happily obliged. When they were both only in their skin, she wrapped her arms around him and hugged him tightly again.

She sighed. "This feels so good."

"Yes it does." Adam replied while fucking her with measured intention. His thrusts getting harder.

A white hot electric current of pleasure passed through their bodies. They breathed in erratic unison. Adam continued to lift her up and down faster and faster. The pressure building between them. Sara leaned back against the wall and put one hand on his chest and the other between their joined bodies. She rubbed her clit, her head falling back against the wall her eyes closed as she stroked herself. She moaned loudly.

Adam's eyes burned with desire as he watched her pleasure herself while he forcefully drove his cock into her.

"Adam!" Sara yelled her legs tightening.

"Come for me!" He begged in a hoarse shout.

"I'm coming!" She screamed. "Adam!"

Wave after wave of pulsing heat coursed through her body. Her skin felt feverish against his.

"Thank god! Oh Fuck!" He pumped into her one final time. His body going still as stone before his orgasm rocked through him like a freight train. They caught their breath together not breaking the embrace.

"Shit... Sara... Now that's a good morning."

Sara could not help but giggle. She pushed her face into his chest and inhaled the divinely masculine scent of him. It was heaven. There was nothing better than this. Neither of them made any effort to move. Sara would have been content to be held by this man for the rest of the day.

"I think we should shower before I drive your bare ass home." Adam spanked her bottom for emphasis.

"This will be the most epic walk of shame in the history of walks of shame." Sara joked.

"But, do you actually feel any?" Adam inquired.

"Shame? Fuck no!" Sara laughed. "I had amazing sex with one hot as hell younger man. I insist you honk your horn the entire way down my street to get the attention of all my neighbors before I get out the car. I would like to bow to a jealous, awestruck audience."

Adam shook his head and chuckled. He finally moved and carried her to the bathroom. Sara spotted her coffee on the dresser and reached for it. Adam angled her toward it. She grabbed it and took a satisfyingly long swig.

Chapter Seventeen

Adam drove Sara home in silence while holding her hand. His thoughts were as dark as the morning. Sara was wearing his blue flannel as a dress with her dressy jacket on top. The sleeves of the flannel folded up so her hands were showing. Their time together was coming to an end. Neither of them knew what to say.

Adam realized he didn't officially have her contact information. They had never exchanged numbers. The only way he had to contact her was to show up at her house or message her through her Facebook profile he'd found. Either way made him seem a bit stalkerish. He didn't want to come off as aggressive or trying too hard. Scaring her off was a big concern.

He glanced down at their hands, contemplating how he could win this woman's heart without pushing too hard. He didn't want to come off like a motherless boy needing a new mommy type. He knew she would assume his interest was only sexual or bordering on weird. He would have to work past those assumptions, somehow. Nothing was coming to mind to naturally keep the connection going.

The longer they sat in silence the harder it was to come up with a conversation starter. Adam's thoughts spiraled, imagining her disgust if she thought he was wanting her to mother him.

That thought propelled him to the biggest problem. If he did convince her his intentions were pure, she would have to know he was a vampire sooner or later. After getting thoroughly attached she would reject him and leave. His chest constricted at the thought.

Sara was already mourning the loss of him. She knew it was over. She swallowed hard. She'd be damned if she let herself cry.

She tried to rally herself. *Be satisfied with what you got. Be thankful for the night of your life.*

The desire to see him again soon was overwhelming, but what would it sound like if she tried to continue the connection. Would he see her as a desperate old woman? Would she be forcing him into an awkward situation that he would have to reject her? She couldn't risk ruining the beautiful time they'd spent together by pushing for more.

Adam finally broke the silence, "So, what do you have planned for Christmas?"

"I always host Christmas Eve. Everyone gets all fancy. Shawn and his family come over. Several friends always pop by and my mom spends the night. I have the bar stocked and everyone brings food. Even though Hazel's too old to believe, Santa still fills stockings and brings presents. We all get really drunk," Sara gushed, relieved he broke the silence. Before she could stop herself the words tumbled out of her mouth, "If you're not busy you should stop by." She regretted it instantly.

One moment of silence too long and Sara was nervously over explaining, "I'm sorry. I overstepped. I know, we don't really know each other and you have been so nice. Oh my god, so nice to me. That was pushing it. I just had so much fun hanging out with you but I don't want you to think I'm trying to be your sugar mama or something…" She trailed off mortified.

Did I really just say, sugar mama?! Sara screamed in her head.

Adam squeezed her hand and released it.

"Sara," He said as he made the turn into her neighborhood.

He pressed his hand down onto his horn. She nearly hit her head on the roof of the Durango, she jumped so high. The sound was unexpected and incredibly loud on a quiet morning.

His face cracked into the biggest smile as he picked his hand off the horn and started to put it back on. Sara's face was incredulous until it finally dawned on her what he was doing.

She squealed "NO!"

Quickly she grabbed his hand before he could honk the horn again. She gasped for air, so surprised by his practical joke. The deep belly laugh coming from Adam was contagious. Sara bent over laughing, tears springing out of her eyes. It took her a minute or two before she could say something.

"You devil!" She barked out between peels of laughter.

"You said you wanted an awestruck audience." Adam, still not under control, seemed pretty proud of his joke.

"Seriously, you're crazy!"

She shook her head at him. Adam grinned back at her. His sparkling mischievous eyes took her breath away. She just stared.

"Adam." Sara began quietly.

Before she could go on he interrupted her, "I would love to stop by Christmas Eve. Thank you for inviting me."

Adam pulled into her driveway and turned off the Durango. They sat contemplating each other.

Sara finally broke the silence "I had a wonderful night and morning."

She reached for the door handle slowly not wanting to leave.

"I did too." Adam replied as he pushed back a lock of hair behind her ear.

He reached out to her with both arms and hugged her. She reciprocated his embrace immediately. He drew back and placed his hands on each side of her face and slowly kissed her forehead. Sara sighed. He kissed her lips firmly. He pulled back and rested his forehead against hers and said earnestly.

"You're a beautiful woman. Thank you for filling my night with joy."

Sara was speechless. The embrace, the kisses and his words were so heartfelt. He released her and she opened her car door.

"Goodbye, I'll see you soon?" She said.

"Yes, you will." He responded.

She got out of the car. The brisk winter breeze blew right up the bottom of her shirt to her bare backside. She shivered and jogged for her front door. She heard the Durango crank up behind her as the front door swung open in front of her.

Hazel, hair disheveled, rubbed her eyes, "Mom!" Hazel looked her up and down.

Sara ran past her into the warm house. Hazel shut the

front door and followed her.

"Mom?!" Hazel questioned.

Sara turned around and took Hazel's hands and started to spin her around in a happy dance. Hazel half participated.

"Oh Hazel." Sara sighed loudly. "It was the most magical night of my life."

"Tell us more, Ms. Hartford!" A boy's voice called out from the couch.

One of Hazel's friends had awakened. Sara smiled in his direction. The living room was strewn with what looked like every blanket and pillow in the house. Two other sleeping lumps of teenager could be seen on the floor. Aside from a few open chips bags and cans of pop on every surface, the house had survived the unsupervised sleepover.

The teenage boy continued, "Hazel showed us the selfie and might I say, mmmm honey he looked delicious."

Sara plopped down beside her daughter's friend Conner on the couch and Hazel followed suit. Conner eyed her morning-after ensemble with a raised eyebrow and pursed lips.

"What?" Sara asked innocently.

"I may not have seen you leave the house last night, Ms. Hartford, but I know you didn't leave in that." Conner giggled. He was loving this.

"Yeah, Mom. Explain yourself." Hazel chimed in.

"It's not my fault." Sara did her best teenage voice. "I like lost my dress."

"Young lady, how did you lose your dress?!" Conner and Hazel said in unison.

The two sleeping teenage lumps on the floor both turned over, yawned with eyes half open listening in on the conversation.

"Hey, I'm a grown-ass-woman and grown-ass-woman-things happened. Forget about the dress. There's no more dress." Sara made a sad face. "I really loved that dress too. What did you guys do last night? I hope you didn't need me for anything."

"Every single parent popped by." Hazel said in an annoyed voice. "Seriously all their mom's dropped by as if they orchestrated the drop in's by the hour. We weren't planning anything weird so hopefully next time you sleep over at a hot guy's place we can be truly unsupervised."

"Ms. Hartford, let's get back to the subject at hand." Conner took control of the conversation. He had decided a year ago he was going to call Sara, Ms. Hartford because he thought it was a quirky thing to do and he never stopped. "I think we still, need to know… What happened to Steve? Also does this new guy have a younger brother cause damn!"

"Adam's an only child and Steve ended up being married." The room made a collective gasp.

"Damn and Dastardly." Conner whispered.

"Yes indeed." Hazel seconded.

"..but then kismet happened. Adam was at the same bar and I desperately needed a ride out of there…"

"That's not the only kind of ride she needed." One of the teenage lumps on the floor quipped.

Sara made a fake disapproving face in its direction while the other teens laughed at her expense. "You shush." She smiled and shook her head. "Adam was the perfect gentleman. If only he were 15 years older…" She trailed off.

Conner patted Sara's leg knowingly. "You're a strong independent woman, Ms. Hartford. Don't let society tell you who you can be with."

"Thanks honey, but you did see him right? It's not just

society that wouldn't understand. I don't even understand how I got the one night. I half expected him to hand me a bill this morning." The teenagers chuckled. "Which I would have gladly paid!" That made them crack up.

"Mom!" Hazel exclaimed.

"OK" Sara said and stood up. "I haven't even dared to check my phone. I bet I have a lot of notifications and replies to make. I'm sure you guys can sleep another few hours. I'm going to go snuggle in my bed and catch up on my scrolling." She left the kids to go back to sleep.

Sara shut the door behind her and climbed into her bed. Through her window she could see the sky beginning to lighten with the impending sunrise. She grabbed her phone out of her purse and checked through the texts. She smiled at the responses from Shawn and Hazel to her selfie with Adam. It was still early, only around seven, but she figured Shawn wouldn't mind the wake up if it included some juicy gossip.

"Truly the most magnificent sexual encounter of my life. Also just got home. Jealous?" She tapped send.

She scrolled up and gazed at the selfie she'd sent him last night. Adam's sexually charged grin made her sigh.

Sara pulled her fluffy comforter up to her chin and snuggled deeper into her bed. Delicious visions of her night and morning flooded her brain. Another sigh escaped her lips. She shook her head to herself.

Her phone chimed. Shawn's text back, "Meet me at noon. Cocktails and lunch at Beaches."

Sara smiled, he was serious about his gossip. Lunch out with drinks was going to be fun. Having the gossip she had to deliver was going to be even better.

Nothing was going to wipe the smile off her face today. Sara opened her Facebook app. She wished she had the balls to post that selfie with Adam to everyone. She decided a few private messages to her best friends would have to do. At least a few people would know just how lucky she got last night. She had several Facebook friends on the East Coast that she knew were well into their mornings and would love to dish.

Chapter Eighteen

Adam walked into his house just before sunrise. Sara's scent still lingered throughout. It was comforting to smell her. He wished she was still here. The place had finally felt like a home when she was inside of it. After so many months living alone, he now realized how missing the feeling of companionship was eating him alive. The house's emptiness now seemed magnified.

He checked his phone on the way to the living room. It was going to be a long day. The night and morning kept replaying through his mind. He definitely wasn't ready to go to sleep just yet. Opening the Facebook app he clicked Sara's name under recent searches. Waffling for a moment he decided to go for it and just clicked, *friend*. He questioned his decision immediately.

Shit.

Whatever. I'm not going to try to play any games. I want her to know I'm in.

Adam stretched out on the sofa and got comfortable. His phone chimed a notification.

That was quick.

Sara had confirmed their online friendship. Adam switched over to messenger and wrote. *"I figured a night together was enough connection to friend you on social* media. I just wanted to say that I had an amazing night with you."

He paused to think. He didn't want to say the wrong thing. He wanted to be charming, to lay the groundwork for continuing their relationship.

"I've never met anyone that I've laughed so much with." He decided short and sweet was the way to go. He ended the message with an emoji heart and clicked send.

Messenger beeped. She'd seen it.

He held his breath waiting. Every second felt like a minute. Would it be a dismissive response? Does she regret inviting him to Christmas? Self-doubt was rearing its ugly head.

What am I, sixteen? Why am I so fucking nervous?

Because yeah... so what, you showed her a good time and that's all she was looking for. She'd never consider a serious relationship with a twenty-four-year-old. He grappled with himself as he waited for her to finish typing.

I'm not twenty-four! Adam yelled in his head.

The dots moved letting him know she was writing back.

Sara wracked her brain for a response. His message didn't really have a question in it to respond to. Her stomach hummed with butterflies.

What do I say?!

Best sex ever thanks?

Oh my god! No.

"HAZEL!!!!!" She screamed.

Sara heard Hazel fall off of the couch and hit the floor, followed by thundering footsteps. Her bedroom door flew open.

"WHAT? Are you okay?!"

"He friended me and he messaged me! He knows I've seen it. I have to respond now!"

"Oh my god." Hazel's eyes were big.

"What do I say?"

"I don't know! CONNER!!"

He was already in the doorway; he covered his ears dramatically and briefly side-eyed Hazel for blasting his eardrums.

"Ms. Hartford, you must have really left an impression on the boy."

"Shut up and help me." Sara read them what Adam had written.

"Whoa." Hazel said. "Mom, he really likes you."

"What? No. I'm too old for him. There's no way a man like that would give up twenty-something models for an almost forty-year-old woman. Seriously. Obviously, it's like a booty call thing. A fun night in his back pocket." Sara was surprised how a twinge of sadness crept in as she said that.

"So what? Why don't you put him in your back pocket too?" Conner rationalized.

"Yeah, Mom. You looked happy this morning. Who cares? You're a modern woman."

"Ms. Hartford." Conner grabbed Sara's shoulders. "Seize your inner sex goddess and put this boy toy in YOUR back pocket." Conner nodded and released her shoulders. "You're in charge here!"

Sara took a deep breath. Who knew teenagers could be such good council.

"You're right. I had the night of my life and why not have that on standby. He's very fun and sweet. The body of a

God! A major step up from Clark."

"MOM!" Hazel was dismayed.

"Oh, Honey. Not even in the same ballpark." Conner shook his head. His face looked like he just ate a lemon. "Not even on the same planet. Not even the same galaxy. Not even the-"

"OK. OK. I get it." Sara interrupted him.

Sara started typing. *"You really know how to show a girl a good time. I'm so happy that bastard Steve ended up being married."* She added a laughing face emoji and three hearts.

"Is that good you guys?" Sara hesitated before hitting send.

"Perfect." The teens said.

Sara tapped send.

Adam let out a sigh of relief. He was happy Steve was a bastard, too.

"Steve's loss was my gain." Adam spoke as he typed. *"I should send him a thank you note. Dear Bastard, Thanks for being such a bastard. She gave one hell of a blow job."* Adam paused "I went too far..." He smiled as he backspaced over that last sentence. He ended his fake letter to Steve, *"Sincerely, The guy who really got lucky."*

He tapped send.

The dots moved immediately. Adam waited anxiously. Her response was quick. *"LOL! We should send that to him with the picture I took of us last night. Really rub his nose in it."*

Adam quickly responded. *"We can send a piece of your green dress with it."* He remembered tearing it off her and his jeans got tighter. He tapped send.

"*Buahaha! My poor dress. Rest in pieces my lovely girl.*" Sara replied.

Conner and Hazel stared at Sara with raised eyebrows and smirks on their faces.

"Get! I have this under control now. Thank you. Bye!!" She dismissed them from her room with a flourish of hand waving.

They giggled as they left, closing the door behind them. Sara returned her attention to her phone screen, waiting impatiently for what he would say next. Giddy, she snuggled back down into her comforter.

"*She made the ultimate sacrifice for us. I'll never forget her or her comrade in arms Private Panties.*" Adam's message appeared on her screen.

Sara laughed out loud. Her belly tightening thinking of that moment this morning. Sex with Adam could become addicting.

"*The glacial breeze on my bare undercarriage gave me quite the wake up this morning. My poor frozen biscuits.*" Sara tapped send.

"*It would be my pleasure to warm those biscuits if you need me to, anytime.*" Adam responded with a winking emoji at the end.

The room definitely felt warmer to Sara. She kicked a leg out from under her comforter. She was having fun. It was like being a teenager again, flirting with a boy.

"*They're heating up just thinking about it.*" Sara added a volcano and a heart eyes emoji. Her breathing shallowed. She bit her lip.

Damn it! If there weren't teenagers in my living room that might hear my vibrator crank up... I could definitely get off right now. It might take a bit, but fingers it is...

Sara put her hand under the comforter and under Adam's soft flannel shirt.

Easy access with Private Panties missing in action. She smiled and softly swept her fingers over herself as she waited for his reply.

Adam took a deep breath. His blood heated and thickened his cock. He considered his reply carefully. He wanted strong, sexy and tantalizing. Not too aggressive. Got to keep it light and safe. He didn't want to throw out any weird vibes.

"Remembering you naked and bent over, searching for those panties this morning is getting my blood warm right now." He tapped the fire emoji and send.

Waiting for her reply was tortuous. He didn't know how each message would be taken and hoped they were both on the same page.

The dots animated. He held his breath waiting for her reply.

"Remembering your hard naked body against me has got me typing with one hand... you can use your imagination for what I'm doing with the other." Pink cheek face emoji at the end of her reply.

Whoa. Yes. This woman!

Adam contemplated his response chewing on his bottom lip. He felt more of his blood flowing south. His heart slowly thumping in his ears. He wanted to turn her on. Make her come imagining him fucking her.

"You're being so naughty right now, making me this hard when I'm all alone. I think I'll be warming up those buns next time with a firm spanking, teach you a lesson. I'll bend you over this couch and slowly fill you with this hard cock." He hoped that was what she was hoping to hear.

No emoji needed on that. Adam tapped send.

Sara's breathing hitched when she read the word spanking. Her fingers danced around her clit. Her pulse pumping in her ears.

Oh, he's good. Damn. That big dick. His chiseled chest. The vivid imagery caused the pressure to swell in her core.

"I've been so bad. A hard cock with no one on their knees in front of it. No wet willing mouth to suck it... to lick the length of it, draw it in the warm depths of my throat. My fingers are soaking wet and I can barely breathe."

That sounds good! Who knew I had such sexting skills? Sara thought.

She focused on sucking his dick last night and contracted her muscles holding her breath until she got lightheaded. She gasped and contracted her abs and kegel muscles even tighter as her fingers entered herself. She put the phone down on the bed beside her pillow and her other hand took over on the clit.

Her phone chimed a notification. She turned her head to read it.

"I'll never forget your hot wet pussy pulsing as you came in my mouth. If you'd continued sucking my dick for a minute longer you would have had felt my cock explode the same way in yours."

Yes! Yes! Oh fuck that did it.

Sara's breath chopped out as each wave jerked through her body. She laid her head back on the pillow. Her heart seemed to be chugging on thick blood in her chest.

"Whew." She sighed and grabbed her phone.

"That got it! God you're good." She tapped the high-five emoji a few too many times. Send.

Adam was grinning ear to ear.

"Glad to be of service, sweetheart. I hope you have a good day." It seemed like the best note to end the conversation on, he tapped send and put his phone down.

He was left with a raging hard on, which only took a minute to stroke into submission.

Chapter Nineteen

The hostess led Sara to an already occupied window table. The riverside bistro was a hotspot during the summer but in the winter it was a ghost town. This time of year only the die-hard regulars still came for the signature cocktails and river views. Shawn stood up when he saw her and initiated a slow clap that dumbfounded all the other patrons enjoying their lunches.

Embarrassed, Sara picked up her pace, literally running to the table. "Quit it!" she said, her eyes big and her smile threatening to escape.

"I bow to the Queen of Cougars. May she roar forever more!" Shawn drawled with a low bow.

"Sit down!" Sara demanded taking her seat.

Shawn chuckled and his eyes danced.

"I heard you may have lost a dress last night. I didn't believe it because I knew that dress was designer and you were wearing it the last time I saw you."

"Hazel's such a gossip!"

"She's our daughter."

"That explains it." Sara nodded.

"So... How was your night?" Shawn steepled his fingers under his chin and waited.

"Absolutely... Fucking... Amazing." Sara stated

shaking her head with a look of disbelief. "I don't know how it happened. I mean I know how it happened, but how the fuck did that happen?"

"From the top, what the fuck happened with Steve?"

"Well, lucky for me he turned out to be married. The son of a bitch. Adam was at the same bar and I had waved him over to say hi which caught the eye of an older couple that just happened to be Steve's in-laws. Obviously that joint is the place to be. We should totally go back there. The drink I ordered was fantastic."

"You digress. Continue."

"Adam swept me away from that embarrassing scene and out into the night. I asked him to share a drink with me."

"Queen."

"Yes indeed." Sara continued. "After making sure he was unattached I might have had an out of body experience and indicated I was down to bone."

Shawn laughed out loud, catching the attention of a nearby table. He waved his hand at them dismissing their attention.

"So... we went back to his place and fucked."

"So the sex was...?" Shawn prompted.

"On another plane of existence."

"...and the dick was?"

"Epic." Sara emphasized using her hands to express herself.

"Nice! I noticed you had a new friend on Facebook."

"He friended me! All I can guess is that he wants pussy on call? I'm as shocked as you are. We had a great time and we laughed a lot, but what is he doing? I don't know." She shrugged.

Their waitress arrived with a tray holding two very

smart cocktails. Shawn gestured that the first drink the waitress took off the tray belonged to Sara. She put the second in front of Shawn.

"Hey guys! Nice to see you again! I'm assuming since you haven't picked up the menus you're going with your regulars?"

"You know us too well." Shawn replied.

"Yes I do." She grabbed the menus off the table and left.

"As long as you don't start making his car payments, I will assume the best. Like he enjoyed you as much as you did him."

"He seems to be taking care of himself just fine. I got no vibes that he was looking for a sugar mama. Although I did tell Hazel I half expected to be handed a bill in the morning." Sara paused.

"Which you would have gladly paid."

"That's what I said! Ok I'm just going to spit this out... I invited him to Christmas Eve!" Sara closed her eyes and made a face that said 'eeeek'.

"What? Really?"

"It just came out of my mouth. I don't fucking know!" Sara put her head down on the table.

"He said yes," answering Shawn's unasked question into the table.

Shawn's eyebrows shot up.

Sara sat up and shook her head. "What the hell is going on?" She rushed to give him all the information. "His parents both died a couple years ago. He was an only child. I felt he needed a place to go."

"So you are a perverted mommy replacement?"

"Shut up!"

"I'm just thinking out loud," Shawn said with a shrug.

"Well, of course that's already crossed my mind. I didn't need you to say it."

"Sorry. That would be pretty gross to find out later, though." Shawn pointed the orange peel swirl from his drink at her before dropping it to the table.

"I know. That would be so embarrassing. I'd rather never know. Maybe after Christmas I'll break off contact. I really don't want to tarnish this whole thing with a realization like that. It was so magical."

"Yes, lets get back to the magical parts." Shawn stated.

Adam woke up to his phone ringing. He shook his head to clear the sleep from his brain. He fumbled around in his blankets and came up with the phone. It was a Facetime from Raphael.

Ugh. Vampires and their love of talking face to face.

It seemed to be a cultural thing. For the old ones, the novelty of technology bringing one face to face across oceans and continents was an amazing accomplishment. Especially to those that had lived through centuries before electricity. Adam tapped *answer* and was greeted with the face of his best friend.

"Hello, brother! Why haven't you called?" Raphael's dark eyes were more than a little hurt.

"Sorry, man. I've meant to, but honestly I think I've been a little depressed up until very recently."

Raphael raised an inquisitive eyebrow. "It looks like you're in your own bed. There's only three days until Christmas. You're not making it to the villa, I take it?"

"No. I'm not."

Adam left it at that even though Raphael was a trusted friend. He wasn't willing to risk Rebecca knowing anything about his personal life.

"Damn. It's definitely not going to be as fun without you. You've really brightened up the villa these past 15 years. I was looking forward to it. "

"Thanks. I'm sorry man. It's been tough. I'll miss seeing you and all the others too. I hope time can smooth this split and we can all go back to being the friends we were. You should really come to the States for a visit. It's been too long. I can transfer those airline tickets Rebecca left me and we could have another epic weekend in Vegas."

Raphael's eyes lit up. "Now that might be interesting. You know how much I've wanted to see Cher's new show. I haven't seen her live since '89."

"You work out the details and I'll meet you there."

"That's a deal." Raphael nodded. "Now I'm excited, but I feel terrible you're spending Christmas alone though. Are you sure you don't want me to take a red eye. I could rent us a cabin. We could spend Christmas roughing it by a lake or something."

Adam smiled, Raphael really would be willing to drop everything for him. "No, man you can't leave everybody hanging like that." Adam knew his friend might not take no for an answer. He decided to confide a small tidbit of current information in hopes of keeping Raphael in Italy. "Seriously, things are really looking up for me."

Adam raised his eyebrows and nodded his head, conveying to his friend that he wasn't going to be as alone as Raphael was assuming.

Raphael slowly smiled, "I see. I'm happy to hear that.

You've been worrying me."

"Tell everyone hi for me and if anyone's in the area don't forget about me." Adam said.

"Will do. See you later, brother."

"Thanks for calling. Later." Adam tapped *end call* and laid back down in his bed.

Vegas with Raphael, that'll be cool. Things are looking up all around.

He had been afraid that once he broke up with Rebecca he would lose all of his friendships. She had introduced him into her circle and all these years they were the only family he had. They were an eclectic lot of vampires. They came from all over the world and any given century.

Adam turned his head to look at the side of the bed that Sara occupied last night. A soft wafting of her scent reached his nose. How wonderful it would be to wake up and not be alone. He had slept the day away. It was time to get up and get ready for a night of Ubering.

He opened his Facebook app to check out if Sara had posted anything new while he had slept the day away. She had been tagged by Shawn in a picture of them smiling at lunch with delicious looking cocktails in hand. Sara looked happy, her beautiful hair pulled over one shoulder. The caption read, *"Nothing better than cocktails and juicy gossip!"* Adam smirked.

I bet they had a lot to talk about. He tapped the love reaction.

Adam's throat ached. He was thirsty. The old familiar feeling in the back of his throat reminding him that he wasn't human. The feeling used to disgust him but over the years he'd just accepted it. The desire for blood stirred memories of last night. Picturing Sara under him, being inside her while tasting the hot liquid… He tried to cancel his dark daydream, his body already responding. He knew of the ecstasy a vampire could feel when their fangs sank into silky, smooth skin. He needed to shut down his brain.

"Stop your psycho thoughts and get fed." He mumbled to himself throwing off the covers and getting out of bed.

He opened the door and walked into a bedroom where his blood supply was stashed. Half of the room was stacked floor to ceiling with various sizes and shapes of cardboard moving boxes. Everything that remained of his parent's life was in this room. He hadn't opened them since he'd packed up their home sixteen years ago.

Adam opened the closet door. It had a deep freeze and mini fridge hidden inside. He opened the fridge. There were about twenty blood donor bags stacked inside. He took out three.

He opened his deep freeze, "Fuck. I'm running low. This is going to suck." It was almost empty but he took three frozen bags and put those into the fridge to defrost.

Adam took the thawed bags over to a towel warmer plugged into the wall nearby. It had several towels folded next to it. He wrapped the towels around the bags and put them into the unit. He set the timer for ten minutes. He'd learned this little trick from a friend. It's not like you can put a blood bag in the microwave. One thing being they were plastic bags, and the other was that it just ruined blood to be reheated that way. A few minutes in a towel warmer and voila, perfect temp.

Adam turned around and looked at the boxes. They had been in storage at his and Rebecca's house. He never had to walk by them. They were out of sight, out of mind.

Here, he saw them every day and it filled him with sadness every time. He had been human when he spent that week alone packing up their home. He didn't want anyone's help doing it, but now he realized how utterly alone that had made him. He wished he'd taken his friends up on their offers to help, but you can't go back in time and be less stubborn.

Automatically reading the labels on the boxes, he saw one of his mother's. It read, "Mom's jewelry making supplies." Adam's mother had been an artist. She made the most beautifully intricate stamped and carved leather. She would make elaborate jewelry or art pieces with the leather.

Adam remembered spending time with her in her workshop growing up. She'd give him strips of leather and he would try to make his own designs. He spent so much time with her that way, both intensely focusing on their own art. Of course, after puberty hit, Adam spent less and less time crafting with his mom and more time out with friends trying to talk to girls.

Adam stepped toward the box before he realized what he was doing. He shook his head. "No." He whispered. His mind wasn't ready to open this box but his heart pulled him another step closer.

Before he knew it he was impulsively ripping it open. The smell of leather hit him like a ton of bricks.

"Mom," he said, the breath knocked out of him.

He picked up the closest unfinished piece with an ornate filigree design embossed on buttery light brown leather. Adam brought it to his nose and inhaled the familiar aroma. The box was filled with supplies and tools along with her unfinished pieces. He dug around, inspecting each item. There was a square fabric covered box underneath a container of stone beads. He lifted it out for a better view.

Adam set the box on the nearest surface and opened it.

"Wow," he smiled.

It was filled with his amateur attempts at leather crafting. The first strip of well-worn black leather he pulled out had "I Love You Mom" in his cursive. It was embossed unevenly with a childlike depiction of a dragon's head breathing fire. She had helped him make it into a bracelet and she'd worn the thing proudly for years.

His heart hurt as he lifted up kid made disaster after disaster. Only a mother could love this awful looking stuff. Adam shook his head and laughed to himself.

"Sorry, I sucked at this. I had no idea."

He went back to the large box and under his cringe-worthy childhood craft projects was a beautifully carved wooden display box. He remembered it was for her finished projects. She'd take it to street fairs and handmade artisan events. Adam carefully lifted it out and set it down. He opened it to find fifteen finished and priced one-of-a-kind pieces of jewelry.

These are so amazing, Mom. You were so gifted.

He picked up a wide leather cuff bracelet and put it around his wrist. A Viking inspired Celtic knot pattern was intricately carved around a fierce wolf. It fit perfectly. He sighed. He could feel the energy and work she'd put into the piece. He turned his wrist back and forth in front of his face, examining it.

The next piece to catch his eye was feminine and had precious gemstones sewn into the delicate design. It made him think of Sara. He would love to give her this for Christmas.

Could I make something beautiful now? He wondered.

The timer chimed on the towel warmer. He had totally

forgotten about his thirst. He grabbed the now very warm towel wrapped blood bags. He drank from one, enjoying the life giving sustenance. It glided down his throat warming his entire body, giving him strength. His mind was alive with memories and new thoughts. He wanted to make a bracelet especially for Sara and his brain bounced back and forth through ideas.

"What would be perfectly her?"

Adam continued to drink and think.

Chapter Twenty

"Mom, you're making me nervous."

Sara stopped herself from biting another fingernail off. She lowered her hand from her mouth.

"Sorry. I'm just not sure what the hell I was thinking."

I'm questioning the choice of impulsively inviting my new 24-year-old lover to our family Christmas! Sara exclaimed in her mind.

Hazel shrugged. "I don't know, Mom. You had a good time with him. You've been chatting on Messenger for the past couple days. You obviously like him. He seems to like you..."

"I wonder why, though?"

"Shut up. Everyone likes you, Mom! You're a charmer and you know it. So what if you're older than him."

"Have you forgotten what he looks like?" Sara asked.

"We've all seen each other, Mom." Hazel loudly rolled her eyes. "You're not a hideous monster because you're thirty-nine. Jesus."

"Okay. Okay. I'll shut up." Sara's silence only lasted a few seconds. "Why is he coming though? Seriously." Sara put her fingernail back between her teeth. Hazel swatted the hand away.

"What time is he supposed to get here?" Hazel asked.

"He said around seven."

"You have an hour. You're dressed. You look beautiful. Food is all set out. You can relax and enjoy," Hazel rationalized.

The doorbell rang a few too many times and a look of panic crossed Sara's face.

"It's just the twins! Seriously, Mom! What are you, sixteen?"

Hazel went for the door as Shawn opened it letting in two very dressed up toddlers, their curly pigtails bobbing up and down.

"Haze!" They yelled in unison running toward their sister. Hazel knelt down and accepted their hugs.

"Merry Christmas!" Shawn yelled from the door. He carried a covered dish of some sort in his hands. Behind him, Ben carried too many packages on his way to the Christmas tree.

"Aunt Say-wa!"

The girls had finished greeting Hazel and were hugging Sara's legs. She bent down and scooped both of them up, one on each hip.

"My sugar pops!!!"

Sara kissed them on their cheeks.

"Merry Christmas! Did you like the lights outside? I added more!"

"Outside!" They both pointed to the door and Sara carried them back to the door to let them see the light display again.

She set them down on the porch. Sara leaned back into the house, grabbed her coat off the hook, and quickly donned it.

She yelled into the house, "Hazel, grab me the green

bag full of cookies for the neighbors. We're going to make our rounds!"

Sara followed the girls around as they ooh and aah'd at her lights. Several cars slowly passed her house and Sara told the twins to wave.

"Here, Mom!"

Hazel practically threw the bag out the front door in her haste to shut out the frigid breeze.

"Hey girls, you want to deliver treats with me?"

"Yeah!!" They said excitedly.

Sara carefully led them across the street to their first stop. The twins ran up to the door, each hitting the doorbell many more times than were needed.

Clark swung the door wide with a cheerful smile, "Merry Christmas, neighbor and friends." He smiled down at the adorable girls.

The girls let him know, "We got tweets!"

Sara lifted out a pretty package with a card on top.

"Your famous Monster Cookies?" Clark asked Sara a tad too excitedly.

"Of course!" Sara replied handing them over.

"I never got to hear about that date you went on. How'd that go?"

"That motherf..." Sara almost forgot she was standing with two toddlers. Who were looking up at her as she spoke. She restarted. "That guy was a boogerface." The girls eyes went wide before they let out giggles.

"Oh really. A boogerface huh?" Clark's inquired.

"Yup a married boogerface." Sara nodded.

"I'm sorry." Clark shook his head. "What a di... I mean, what a total... stink bottom."

Sara laughed. "Yeah total. Hope you have a great

Christmas. I've got a few more cookies to deliver. See you later!"

"Bye, girls!"

Clark had already started opening the cookie box before he closed the front door.

Adam finished tying a bow on the box. It held the bracelet he had made for Sara. His countertop was strewn with all his mother's tools and several discarded attempts. He was happy with the final product. He had spent two days honing his skills with his mother's tools. His vampire strength enabled him to barely lean into the leather to emboss it. With his keen eyesight and precision reflexes, he was able to focus in on fine details. He knew his mom would be proud.

"I hope she likes it," he said to himself.

He added the box containing the bracelet to the bag of additional gifts he was bringing with him. He knew how to get people to like him and that was best accomplished quickly with gifts. He had something for everyone he knew would be there. He was prepared to woo them all. Adam knew that acceptance from her clan would be the best way into her heart.

Tonight would make or break his entry into her life. If he fit comfortably into her family circle, how could she say no?

"I've got to be charming and likable. I can do that right. Right?"

"Granny, did you hear mom has a 'friend' coming tonight?" Hazel's fingers lingered in their air quotes as she wiggled her eyebrows at her grandmother. Sara's family stood around her food laden kitchen island, happily stuffing their faces while they chatted.

"Your gossipy nature is getting out of hand!" Sara side-eyed her. "I was just about to tell her."

"You sure are pushing it to the last minute, Mom." Hazel replied.

"Oh, really? Do tell. Your gossipy nature is one of my favorite things about you." Sara's mother's attention was on Hazel.

The doorbell rang.

"Looks like you're going to get to meet him right now..." Hazel could barely contain her giddy smile.

"He's here! Holy shit." Sara exclaimed. She turned around in a circle, seemingly unable to function.

Hazel and her Granny exchanged looks. Hazel was going to enjoy this reveal. Shawn and Ben joined in on the look exchange. The house went silent except for two oblivious toddlers squirreling about and the Christmas music playing in the background.

Sara looked at her mother and quickly said, "OK, so he's young. I know that. Be open-minded. We're just friends. He's a very sweet man. Don't say anything weird. That goes for all of you." Sara looked pointedly at everyone. "He needed a place to go on Christmas." She walked away.

Sara nervously checked herself in the full-length ornately framed decorative mirror on the way to the front door. She looked into her eyes, they were bright with anticipation. She leaned in and checked her teeth. All clear. She breathed loudly and pushed her shoulders back.

Oh my god. Oh my god, repeatedly tumbled through her head. She swung open the door and there he was, as devastatingly handsome as she had remembered.

"Oh my…" She said. Her knees buckled a little but she caught herself and pretended to bounce and shiver from the cold breeze that flew in the door. He wore a buttery soft light blue flannel and snug jeans. It was thirty-three degrees outside.

"Where's your jacket?"

Sara cringed at her motherly tone.

Oh my god, shut up. She thought.

Adam didn't respond to her question and continued to stand in the doorway. He smiled down at her and said, "Merry Christmas."

"Merry Christmas to you, too." Sara smiled back at him. They exchanged knowing looks. His green eyes were sparkling with sexual energy. She just looked up at him studying the sharp line of his jaw and sensual smirking lips. He raised an eyebrow at her and waited.

"Oh! Yes, please come in."

She finally moved aside and swung her arm wide in welcome.

Adam nodded to her and stepped through the doorway. He extended his arms to her. Sara immediately stepped into his hug. He squeezed her and lifted her off her feet.

"I missed you." He whispered in her ear. Sara squeezed him hard in return. He put her back on her feet.

He missed me? Really?

"Where should I put these?" Adam said indicating the bags he held in one hand. One was filled with brightly wrapped packages and the other was filled with booze. "I figured you wouldn't want anything I could cook. Booze is always a failsafe."

"Good thinking. The gifts can go under the Retro Tree. I have a couple themed trees." She nervously laughed. "I'm a little extra for Christmas, I can't help it." She walked him into the living room that held the aptly named Retro Tree.

"If the 80's were a Christmas tree this would be it," Adam said in appreciation of her handiwork. "This is pretty *rad*."

Sara smiled at his 80's slang. He put his bags down beside it and inspected the plastic candy garland. Every ornament was at least thirty years old. He tilted an ALF ornament toward himself to get a better look. Presents were piled and overflowing beneath it.

"Thank you." Sara beamed. She took a lot of pride in her 80's tree. It was her favorite. It was so perfectly tacky.

The twins ran around the corner, coming to a screeching halt when they saw Adam. He smiled at them and knelt down. "Hello, girls."

The girls slowly walked toward him, their eyes wide.

"Hey girls! This is my friend, Adam. Adam this is Marley and Madison," said Sara.

"I knew I was going to be meeting two princesses tonight so I made sure to bring offerings."

Adam smiled at them and they smiled back. They eyed him as he put his hand into the bag and brought out the first present. They may not have known what the word offering meant right away but they did when they saw the wrapped gift. They clapped their hands. He handed it to Marley, grabbed the second present and handed it to Madison. They squealed and exchanged happy glances with each other.

"You're good." Sara whispered.

Adam looked up at her and grinned. She watched him closely. He was really charming them.

The girls ripped open the wrapping paper to reveal cute plush puppies wearing Santa hats. They hugged the festive puppies tight and showed each other.

"What do you say, girls?" Sara prompted.

"Tank you!!" They shouted and both hugged Adam before running off to show their dads. Adam stood up.

"They are adorable." He stated. "I'm guessing everyone's in another room waiting for us to make an awkward entrance?"

"You guessed right."

"Shall we get it over with?"

"No. Let's hide in here." Sara pretended to hide behind the Christmas tree with her hand out to Adam to join her.

His eyes shimmered reflecting the tree's lights. He took her hand and pulled her toward him. Sara was surprised by the tug and stumbled into his firm muscular chest. Her heart picked up its pace in anticipation.

"Do you regret inviting me?" Adam asked softly. His arms enveloped her and his chin rested on the top of her head.

Sara heard the vulnerability in his voice and rushed out, "No! Of course not, I'm just nervous. You're.... you."

She fumbled that. She tried to course correct. "I'm... me." She failed.

"Yes and..." Adam prompted.

"No one will understand why you're bothering with me." Sara decided on honesty. "I don't even understand."

Adam leaned back and tilted her chin up with his hand. "I guess I can best explain that by saying. You're... you." He booped her on the nose, his smirk exposed his white straight teeth. He leaned down and kissed her soundly on the mouth.

Adam released her chin and stepped away, her hand still in his.

"Take me to your people."

"Let's not forget the booze. I'm gonna need it."

Sara grabbed the bag before leading Adam to the kitchen.

They entered the very silent kitchen, hand in hand. The only one totally unprepared for Adam was Sara's mom. Her mouth fell open. Hazel, always the helpful teenager, reached over and assisted in closing it with an upward tap to her Granny's chin. That made Sara start to giggle. In turn Hazel began to cackle.

Adam shook his head at them. Shawn took over where the ladies of the house were failing and started the introductions.

"I'll make the introductions that I'm responsible for, I guess." He looked mock stern at Sara who hadn't recovered from laughing at her mom's shocked face. "It's nice to finally meet you, Adam. I'm Shawn. This is my husband Ben and you've met our youngest daughters." Shawn and Ben both shook Adam's hand. Sara gathered herself and put down the bag of booze on the counter.

"Adam, this is my daughter Hazel, and my mom, Pam." Sara completed the introductions.

"Nice to meet you," Hazel and Pam said in unison then looked at each other and giggled.

Sara rolled her eyes.

"Very nice to meet you as well." Adam replied.

Shawn helped himself, sifting through the newly arrived bag of booze. He unloaded a handle of Tito's vodka, a six-pack of ginger beer and limes. He nodded his head in approval.

"Adam, I like how you roll. Let's make some mules!" Shawn exclaimed and proceeded to grab glasses from the cabinet.

Sara breathed a sigh of relief. Something to keep everyone busy for a few minutes would be a perfect way to ease Adam into the mix.

Especially if we all just get really drunk, she thought.

Ben and Shawn busied themselves playing bartender.

"So, how did you guys meet?" Pam directed her question in their direction.

Sara spoke up first, "You know how Hazel is driving now. She needs the car on the nights she stays at Shawn's. I happened to luck out getting a ride from this guy." Sara quickly recognized the double entendre and continued. "He happened to be my Uber driver. We really hit it off..." Sara trailed off.

"And it was such a fun *ride* she invited you for Christmas?" Pam asked with the most innocent of expressions. Sara looked dumbfounded.

"Granny, how else do you thank someone for a five star *ride*?" Hazel bit her lip and stared down her grandmother. They both busted up laughing at the same time.

"You guys! I'm sorry. They are terrible teases. Nothing they say is serious! There is a fifty year age difference but you wouldn't know it by how they act." Sara shook her reddened face. She didn't know how Adam would take being the butt of a joke.

Adam grabbed Sara's hand, "What can I say, it was a Christmas-invite-worthy *ride*."

Shawn choked on the first swallow of his fresh drink. He turned around and made eye contact with Sara. They'd known each other so long he didn't need to speak. He liked that retort and he was an Adam fan now. Sara smiled back at him.

"Mules all around!"

Shawn held out a drink for Adam while holding up his own in the other. Adam took the drink and clinked it with Shawn's.

"Cheers," they said in unison.

Ben handed Sara and Pam fresh drinks. Sara took a long swig.

"I wouldn't mind watching *A Christmas Story*. How about you guys?" Sara suggested. "It's a tradition. Have you ever seen it Adam?"

"More times than the Bumpuses have hounds," Adam responded smiling.

Chapter Twenty-one

Adam curled a finger around a lock of Sara's chestnut hair. They were nestled into her overstuffed sofa. The living room was alive with delighted laughter and Christmas cheer. Everyone was enjoying *A Christmas Story* while they sipped their drinks and cracked wise. The twins kept Shawn and Ben on their toes as they ran wild around the house, coming out of rooms holding random things with which they weren't supposed to be playing.

Adam felt at home. It was so nice he wanted to sigh, but held it in. This was a family. This was exactly what he wanted. He had watched this movie every year with his parents. His mom and dad would sit together snuggled on the couch. They were a happy couple his entire life. He had assumed he would find a woman that would be his best friend and companion just like they had. Right now, he was certain he had found it. He would do anything to win her and this life.

"I can't believe you don't have a leg lamp in your window," Adam said surveying the room, just in case he'd missed it. Every surface was livened up with Christmas cheer.

She really has a knack for making things pretty, he thought.

"I know, right?! I say I'm getting one every year and then never do. But I wouldn't settle for anything less than the full size replica and they are like two hundred and fifty dollars. But I did buy pink bunny pajamas for Hazel when she was five," Sara replied.

"Oh my god, I forgot about those!" Hazel exclaimed. "Why did I have to grow out of those? I would totally be wearing them right now."

"I'm going to set a reminder in my phone for next December, so I remember to find a pair for you." Sara pulled her phone out. Adam smiled down at her and watched her set it.

"Yes!" Hazel clapped her hands.

"I need another one of these drinks. That was fantastic," Pam stated to the room.

"Refills all around," Shawn said and stood up. He took a glass from Pam.

Adam stood up and took Sara's cup. He intended to chat up Shawn. Having the best friend on his side was paramount to his acceptance into Sara's clan.

"Mmm, a handsome bartending assistant. I'll take it." Shawn teased.

"Don't get any ideas," Sara teased him right back.

Ben raised an eyebrow at Shawn and said. "He couldn't handle you, baby."

Adam smirked, having experienced his fair share of flirty gay men in his life. He replied to Shawn suggestively, "You pour. I'll stir."

He winked at Sara. She shook her head at him.

"You're bad." Shawn laughed.

Adam followed him into the kitchen and put the glasses on the counter. Shawn refilled them with ice from the dispenser.

Shawn turned around from the refrigerator with a

purpose in his eyes. He looked up at Adam, making direct eye contact when he said, "You know I've loved Sara for 20 years?"

Adam nodded, "Yes, she's told me."

Adam knew this was coming. He expected someone would question his motives. He was ready.

"We are soulmate best friends for life."

Adam nodded.

"There's no one as kind as Sara. There's no one as genuine."

Shawn paused for Adam to nod his agreement. "All I can hope is that you are a good person who isn't trying to get something from her or play her foul. She doesn't deserve that. She deserves this escapade with you. Girl, is sparkling over this. But I'm warning you. Don't play her. She doesn't deserve any ulterior motives or a broken heart. So I'm begging you, if you do have some underlying fucking bullshit you're weaving, just stop now and break it off. Believe me, you don't want the karma that would come from hurting her. She's beloved by the gays and we are everywhere."

Adam smiled and didn't break eye contact with Shawn as he contemplated what he would say.

"Shawn, It's going to sound farfetched and you might not believe me now. That's fine, I hope to have plenty of time with Sara to prove myself. She is all I want. I have no sneaky motives other than trying to get everyone in her family to like me so that maybe she'll look past my... youth." He indicated his young face. "and want to be with this..." Adam put his hand over his heart.

Shawn tilted his head, digesting what Adam had said. His eyes softened.

"Hmmm OK. I'll give you the benefit of the doubt. Sara

is having the time of her life with you. I don't want to see that end any time soon."

Shawn took a moment.

"Don't disappointment me." He moved past Adam and poured the first drink. He handed it to him and suggestively said, "Now let's see you stir."

Sara watched Shawn and Adam leave the room. She could imagine her mom's expression and didn't want to turn her head to confront it. She let out a loud breath and slowly turned her to meet the expectant gaze of her mother.

"So..." Pam began but didn't continue.

"Yup." Sara responded.

"I've never been more proud of you." Pam nodded earnestly.

Hazel slapped her knee and fell out.

"Thanks, Mom." Sara rolled her eyes and shook her head.

"I mean, Damn! That is a specimen. I'm going to have to look into this Uber thing." Pam looked to Hazel. "Why was I the last to know? Honestly, that part stings a bit," Pam said dramatically and put her hand over her heart.

"I'm sorry, Granny," Hazel said, contrite. She looked toward Sara with blame in her eyes.

"How much do we know about this fine ass looking man in the kitchen alone with my husband?" Ben pointedly interjected. "I mean I don't want to sound insecure, but we all sure he's just into mature older women right?"

"I don't know. He seemed pretty straight to me." Sara smirked.

"He better keep his stir stick to himself..." Ben

muttered. He glanced toward the doorway they left through.

Sara just ignored him and tried to console her mom for being left out.

"As you can see there's a bit of a discrepancy in age... I didn't expect to ever be introducing him to anyone. I really thought it was a one-night thing. I mean really, what is happening here? I have no idea." Sara put up both her hands in a gesture of her complete lack of clues.

"Did you see his biceps? Those shoulders? I'm going in there... I'll stir my own man's drink, thank you very much."

Ben stood up with a flourish and walked to the kitchen. Everyone left in the room shook their heads with good-natured eye rolls.

"How was the night?" Pam inquired with wide eyes and peaked eyebrows.

"It was spectacular," Sara sighed.

Hazel and Pam exchanged looks.

"We laughed all night too. I know it's weird that he's so young and we can get along so well. He seems to be quite obsessed with 80's and 90's culture. So much so, that he gets all my jokes. I know why I'm enjoying the hell out of this affair. He's the hottest man I've ever seen in real life. I'm not sure what he's thinking dating me, though."

Sara paused, her insecurities rising to the surface of her mind. She shook it off and continued.

"I blurted out the Christmas invite before thinking and was surprised he jumped on it like he did. He doesn't have any family and I feel a loneliness in him. The thought of him spending Christmas alone made my stomach hurt. You know how I am, Mom."

"Yes, I know how you are. He seems genuinely nice." Pam said. "You deserve an affair to remember for a lifetime.

That man in there is definitely unforgettable. I say enjoy the hell out of him. You're not stupid. If all of a sudden he's asking for rent, dump his ass. Unless the dick is worth some rent..."

"Granny! Young ears, here."

Hazel covered her ears with her hands for emphasis.

"A few months for sure," Sara joked as she heard the boys returning.

Pam reached over for a quick high five. Sara obliged.

Shawn and Ben entered the living room with smiles on their faces. She wished she could have been a fly on the wall in there. Obviously, Adam had charmed Ben. He was laughing at something that had been said. Adam followed them, taking up the entire doorway. The light from the kitchen put his muscular frame and trim waist on display. She remembered her hands gliding down those abs and her heart picked up its beat.

Adam made eye contact with her and gave her a devilish smile. The memory of being held against a wall while they fucked flashed in her mind and a shiver of pleasure sparked deep in her belly.

"Someone press play," Shawn playfully commanded. He handed Pam a fresh drink and took his seat.

Adam handed Sara her glass. Sara scooted over to make room for Adam to sit back down. He draped his arm around her and Sara noticed his leather bracelet peeking out from his shirtsleeve. She'd seen leather pieces of this artistic caliber in fancy boutiques. She grabbed his wrist and turned it in front on her face, examining the Viking motif.

"This is really cool." She said. "Where did you get it?"

"My mother made it. She was a very talented leather craftswoman," Adam replied. "I just recently found it in her things."

Oh shit.

Sara could kick herself for inadvertently bringing up his mother.

"It's lovely." Luckily, Sara was saved from herself as the movie resumed in the background and the wise-cracking merriment continued.

The movie's credits rolled. Adam looked down at Sara and she was already looking at him. He tightened his arm around her and she smiled, her blue eyes sparkling with buzzed Christmas cheer. Her joyful expression filled his heart with warmth. So far he was feeling pretty good about how the night was going.

"Let's open some presents!" Sara exclaimed.

"Presents!" Marley and Madison yelled in unison.

The twins who had been paying them no mind suddenly had very good hearing. They clapped their hands. Hazel jokingly mimicked them, clapping her hands in agreement.

"Begin the distribution!" Sara instructed Hazel.

Hazel went to work separating out the gifts from under the tree. She handed them to the twins and told them whom they belonged to. Adam watched the family pretend to shake and guess what was in each box that was put in their pile. He hoped the presents he brought further ingratiated himself into this clan.

Hazel delved into the bag from Adam and came out with a gift with her name on it.

"He's a smart dude." She said under her breath.

Adam smiled to himself. He was the only one that

could have heard her.

Yes, I am one smart dude. He thought. *Teenage daughter's approval makes or breaks a plan to infiltrate a single mother's domain.*

Sara smiled at Adam when Hazel put a gift from his bag onto her pile. She grabbed the box.

"You didn't have to buy me anything." She said. "But I'm glad you did. I do enjoy presents."

"I didn't buy it. I made it." His voice tinged with pride.

"Oh, really?" Sara replied, her eyes intrigued.

Everyone's ears perked to their conversation.

"Start the night, Sara. Open it!" Shawn had no problem putting her on the spot.

"Open it! Open it!" Everyone chanted and the twins joined in.

Sara's face bloomed with blush as she nervously picked at the paper, giving everyone a look that obviously meant "shhhh!"

Adam waited anxiously. The pressure was on. Everyone was watching. If a vampire's palms could sweat, his would be right now. He could hear Sara's heart pounding. She carefully removed the metallic wrapping paper on the rectangle box. She held it for a second before taking a deep breath.

She removed the box's top. Her eyes widened.

"What did he make?!" Shawn's enthusiasm was apparent.

"It's beautiful." Sara reverently whispered. She just looked at the bracelet. "You made this?"

Adam nodded his reply.

Sara was really at a loss for words. The bracelet was a

piece of art. The light sable-colored leather cuff was intricately carved, or embossed. She didn't even know. It looked like a piece of antique lace was imprinted onto it. Tiny gemstone beads were placed at accent points in the design. Two words read "*Lumiere Brillante*" in scrolling cursive script.

"I don't know what to say..." Sara explained.

"You're killing us here. What did he make you?" Shawn spouted out, breaking through her befuddled thoughts.

"It's simply wonderful." Sara said. "Do you sell these somewhere?"

Adam picked the bracelet up out of the box and put it around her wrist. It fit perfectly.

"I was inspired recently to look through some old boxes I have stored. I happened upon a box of all my mother's leather craft supplies and her remaining pieces. I found some very rudimentary pieces I had made with her when I was a young boy. I got inspired and really I think somehow I just channeled her. I messed up a fair amount of leather until I got the hang of it again. I finally created one that is you."

The whole room was listening. Even the twins seemed transfixed by Adam's deep voice. They were standing right by his knee trying to get a look her present. Sara's heart thumped in her hot ears.

"Thank you." Sara said her heart in her eyes.

"Let me see it!" Shawn couldn't contain his curiosity.

Sara didn't want to unsnap it to hand it to him. Instead she stood up and walked over to stand in front of where he sat.

"Whoa, Adam. This is like something you'd find at a high-end boutique behind glass made by an artisan. This is incredible."

He twisted her wrist around to examine it.

Shawn read, "Lumiere Brillante. What does that mean? Lumiere is the candle stick in *Beauty and the Beast* and brillante?"

Adam chuckled. "It translates to, "Bright Light." Those words kept repeating in my head as I made it. It was the perfect description of how I see Sara."

The room was silent for a moment. Sara's breath was caught in her chest. It was the sweetest thing anyone had ever said about her. She swallowed hard.

"It's exactly her." Shawn looked into Adam's eyes pointedly and nodded.

"Awww! OMG!" Hazel gushed. "I wanna see. I wanna see!"

Pam was giving Sara a wide-eyed look that Sara interpreted as her approval.

"Open presents?!" asked the twins in unison.

They had finally lost interest and their patience. They needed to open some presents. Sara returned to her seat, threading her fingers through Adam's. She squeezed.

She was at a loss. What was happening? His gift was thoughtful and beautiful. She'd never received such a meaningful gift from a man before. It made her nervous. Almost scared. It also made her heart reach for him. She looked over at him with eyes full of questions. He looked down at her and answered them with a quick kiss on top of her head.

Chapter Twenty-Two

Adam hated to leave, but he knew the night was coming to an end. He wanted to make sure he didn't overstay his welcome.

Leave them wanting more, he thought.

He was standing in the kitchen with Sara and Hazel. They were all stuffing their faces with Christmas treats. Adam slowly chewed a bite of chocolate covered toffee. It was delicious. Almost as delicious as he knew Sara would be.

Cancel that thought. He forced himself to redirect.

He was completely pleased with how the evening had played out. Sara seemed truly touched by his gift. He watched her, even now, touch it lovingly.

His gift for Hazel seemed to win her over and he'd made the adults laugh when he'd explained to Hazel, "These are called compact discs. People used to put them in CD players to listen to music." She'd given him a classic teenage eye roll.

He'd told her, "Sara said you enjoyed *The Presidents* so much that I thought you might like a crash course in early nineties hits."

She had flipped through the selection: *Nirvana's Nevermind*, *Green Day's Dookie* which made Hazel raise an eyebrow and question, "Dookie? Really?"

Shawn had gasped, "Dookie! That brings back memories!"

"Eww, Dad that sounds wrong." She continued reading off the CD cases, "*Pulp Fiction* soundtrack, *Weezer*, *Korn*, *Tool*, interesting names for bands…"

Shawn, Ben and Sara all were nodding their heads as she read the names.

"Garth Brooks? He looks… interesting," she politely lied.

"Garth Brooks! Oh my god he was HUGE in the nineties!" Sara explained. "Adam that's so funny! I'm going to enjoy these."

Hazel had given her mom a "these are mine" warning look.

Hazel's phone now chimed as she stuffed her face with homemade fudge. She grabbed two cookies off of a plate and left the room abruptly.

"Kids these days." Sara joked.

Now that they were finally alone, Adam seized his opportunity to grab her around the waist and pull her toward him. Her cheeks pinked up in response and she let out a sexy little gasp. He wrapped his arms around her and lowered his head into her neck, letting his teeth graze the skin. The feel of skin against his teeth made blood rush to his cock. He ran his sensitive teeth lightly back and forth letting the blood longing sensations cascade through his body.

He kissed her neck, slipping his tongue along the trail his teeth had taken. Sara shivered in his arms, her head falling away to expose more of her neck to his pleasurable assault. She had no idea what a temptation she presented.

Adam raised his head from her neck, "Regretfully, I should really get going. I bet I can get a couple of fares tonight. People tip generously during the holidays."

Sara leaned back to look at him, her face in a pout, eyes cloudy with arousal. "I don't want you to leave."

"Do you think I made a good first impression with your family?" Adam asked, changing the subject.

"They are smitten." Sara said.

"Are you?" His eyes twinkled.

"You have no idea." Sara smiled. She sighed shaking her head. "Honestly. I'm getting very nervous about how smitten I am. I don't know how dating works these days. I don't know how to play games or be coy. And... are we dating? I don't know. I know I like you. It's scary. You're too young for me and if I get all attached... you could really break this mature woman's heart."

Her eyes were sad as she ended her statement.

Adam leaned in slowly and kissed her. She tasted like honeyed gin and ginger. Adam heard her heart speed up and his body reacted. He wished he could fuck her brains out right there in the kitchen. He deepened the kiss. Electricity flowed through him. He knew he needed to break the contact before someone walked in. He ended the kiss, his hands holding the sides of her face. Her lips were slightly swollen and thoroughly kissed. Her eyes shimmered.

"Sara, I'm not playing a game."

Adam rubbed his thumb across her bottom lip. "I'll prove it to you with time. I've got all the time in the world."

She didn't know how true that really was, but for now he knew he needed to leave this perfect night as is and let her have time with her family without him. Time for them all to process the evening and gossip about him.

"Thank you for a wonderful Christmas Eve." He gave her a simple peck on the lips.

"I wish you would stay," Sara said with big blue puppy dog eyes.

He didn't answer, but took her hand and led her back into the living room. Everyone turned to look at them.

"I can't thank you guys enough for including me in your Christmas. I had a great time tonight. I'm going to get going and hopefully catch a few Ubers tonight."

"It was nice to meet you, man," Shawn gushed. "We are going to enjoy the hell out of that Nintendo Classic. That was fucking awesome. So glad you already had one." He gave Adam a handshake and pulled him into a manly, back slapping hug.

Adam had given them one of the mini video game systems that had been rereleased. He'd gotten one for himself months ago. Luckily, a friend had sent him another one for Christmas. Obviously, he knew what another forty-year-old man might enjoy. It was the perfect re-gift.

Everyone said their goodbyes and Adam collected his present from Sara. The sweetheart had gotten him four dishes, four bowls and all the basic kitchen utensils you could ever need. She'd also gotten him a basic cookbook geared toward dudes. His empty kitchen must have bothered her. He couldn't help but smile as he picked up the box.

Sara walked him to the door. In the foyer Adam turned around to face her. He knew he needed to secure some future plans with her.

"Can I take you out this weekend?"

"Actually I was thinking..." Sara paused.

Adam held his breath anticipating his worst fears that she was about to let him down.

"Yes?" He urged.

"...Hazel will be at her Dad's house this weekend.

Maybe *we* could have a slumber party?"

Sara looked up at him expectantly.

Adam began breathing again.

Yes! He celebrated in his head. *Victorious!*

He smiled and said, "A slumber party huh? That sounds fabulous. Can we do each other's hair and play Truth or Dare?"

"Definitely Truth or Dare," Sara smiled suggestively.

Adam set his gifts down and drew her in for a goodbye hug. He leaned back and tilted her face up to him. He was going to leave her wanting more. His lips descended slowly. She went up on her tiptoes to meet him halfway. The kiss consumed them both. Adam's blood ignited. His intention to leave her wanting more was working on himself. He wished he could throw her over his shoulder and take her to bed right now. His tongue danced with hers. The atmosphere seemed to swirl around him. He rocked his pelvis forward pressing himself to her soft body. She melted into him, moaning into his mouth.

He rubbed his erection against her for emphasis and said, "Consider me RSVP'd."

Sara walked back into the living room on a cloud. Everyone stopped what they were doing and looked at her expectantly. She pranced to the nearest overstuffed chair and pretended to faint into it dramatically, with the back of her hand touching her forehead to add to her pretense.

"GIRL!" Shawn exclaimed. "I'm shook."

Sara smiled and sat up quickly, her faint over. She was bubbling over with a new energy. Her face felt warm and she could still feel his kiss on her lips.

"I know!" She replied.

"He is sex on a stick." Pam stated.

Everyone nodded agreement.

"Merry Christmas to you, Queen." Ben added.

"Am I crazy for even getting involved at all with a twenty-four-year-old? Even if it is merely sexual in nature. I mean I'm not going to stop now. No way, but I just want to know if you think I'm crazy?" Sara excitedly rambled.

"You're trying to tell us it's "merely sexual?" Please!" Shawn, always the straight shooter.

"Mmmhmm." Pam quipped.

"Shit. Okay I'm crushing." Sara admitted.

"Not just you, honey," Ben added.

Shawn shot him a questioning look.

"Not me, baby. I'm saying him to her. A handmade gift..."

Another "Mmmhmm," came from Pam.

Sara touched the bracelet on her arm and her eyes drifted up into a daydream.

"You got it bad, Mom." Hazel said shaking her head.

Sara sighed. "You guys... What in the world is going on?"

"A Christmas miracle?" Pam offered with a nonchalant shrug.

"Yes!" Hazel agreed.

"You don't look a gift horse in the mouth." Pam paused for dramatic affect, "You ride him."

The room cracked up at Granny's bawdy joke.

"Mom! You dirty old bird!" Sara smiled. "I mean that's the plan and everything."

"I've never been more proud." Pam replied with her hand over her heart. "The boy was very likeable. I don't really know any twenty something men that are worth talking to, but he was charismatic. I did like him for more than that face and boy oh boy that body."

"Mmmm those shoulders," Ben sighed.

"Those eyes…" Shawn added.

"That ass." Pam finished.

They giggled.

"You guys! Seriously! Let's keep this Christmas going. Hazel go put on Gremlins. I need a fresh drink."

Sara got up in a flourish and went toward the kitchen.

Chapter Twenty-Three

Rebecca's stilettoes clacked angrily with every step. The sound echoed off the ornately painted ceramic tile floor, punctuating her ire. She stalked toward the open French doors. The frigid night air did nothing to cool her boiling blood.

The generous balcony overlooked Lake Garda. When she reached its edge, she looked down on picturesque villas topped with terracotta roofs. The full moon's beauty reflected across the calm lake.

Explaining Adam's absence to their friends was an ego drain she was not accustomed to. They all really liked him. He was a genuine friend. They all enjoyed his wit. There was a freshness about him even after 15 years. He was still the youngest of all of them. She could feel the undercurrent of disappointment. If they were to choose between the two of them, she wasn't sure it would go her way.

Rebecca's breathing was erratic. Her thoughts just as frantic.

She had known many of these vampires for hundreds of years. Over those centuries, they had evolved together. Lifelong friends, and that meant something to vampires. They were family.

Almost all distinguished Elders now lived to the

standards of the current culture. They lived in stealth, no longer killing to satisfy their hunger. Well, if they did, they did a better job of covering it up. Old habits did die hard.

Rebecca would know. Her penchant for violent satisfaction was what had started the rift between her and Adam in the first place. She rolled her eyes just thinking about his reaction to finding out she still hunted fresh. What a disappointment twenty-first century men could be. So sensitive.

She could feel a spark of rage deep in her chest. Familiar and comforting, she welcomed it. Adam was not the first man she'd turned and brought into her inner circle. She had hoped he was finally The One. No more failed relationships. He was her match. She had never seen a more beautiful man. She wanted him with an intensity she had never felt before.

The two men before him had been prizes to be sure, but Adam, he was magnificent. She'd known he was the one the moment she saw him. He had to be her lifemate. He belonged to her. He was all she'd ever wanted. He equaled her in beauty and together they would have it all. They would be envied.

Everyone knew he had left her. Embarrassment stoked the fire until her chest felt like a furnace. Shame was not an emotion Rebecca dealt with well. An embarrassed child might lash out and hurt someone but an embarrassed vampire... someone might die tonight.

How could he do this to me? After everything I've given him!

Rebecca's hands gripped the railing. Her fingers sunk into the thick wrought iron. There was only one thing that would get her through the rest of this night and that was pulsing in veins inside all the surrounding villas.

She tapped into her instincts letting everything fall away but the need to hunt. The hot, thick pulses in the homes below began to thrum in her ears. Five different hearts beat in the house next door. Two of those were fast like little birds. She knew those were young. She honed into the rhythm. Less than four years old, both of them. Her mouth watered.

Think! You cannot hunt this close to the villa.

Rebecca hopped over the railing and landed 30 feet below onto a soft manicured lawn. She began to run. The anticipation of what was to come filled her with euphoria. She ran like a gazelle, her long legs gliding over the earth. Her heels barely tapping the ground as she bounded faster and faster across the city. Most families were inside for the night. She hadn't come across anyone out alone. She kept going. The further out she went, the less likely anyone at the villa would suspect she had hunted tonight.

She finally pulled back on her pace and surveyed her surroundings. She focused on what she could smell and hear. She heard stirrings around her. Doors being opened. Happy families began to leave their homes. Families that were boisterous from hours of wine and celebrating Christmas Eve. It was time to go to midnight mass. The neighborhoods had begun to come alive.

"Perfecto," Rebecca muttered as she moved toward the sounds.

The home to her right caught her attention. Inside she heard the pounding of four healthy hearts; a man, a woman, and two small children. She could tell their position close to the front door. She heard them telling their children it was time to go.

Rebecca continued up the walkway. She scanned her

surrounding with night vision and hearing so precise she knew no one had seen her. They were almost ready to open their front door. She quickly used a small blade she kept hidden and made several small cuts, one on her temple and two on her arms that bled before closing up leaving behind evidence of foul play. She raised her hand to pretend to knock at the same time the door was opened.

The man, dapper in a hat and scarf, his wife and two daughters in matching skirts and black wool coats stood in their doorway. The husband, startled by her standing so closely in the doorway with her hand raised, automatically smiled. Everyone always smiled at Rebecca. Her face was beautiful and people usually stared. They were never frightened of her. Why would you fear an exquisitely dressed woman with a face like hers?

"Buon Natale" Rebecca said in a perfect Italian accent.

They all replied in kind. The man quickly noticed the blood running down the side of her face. She rubbed her arms feigning she was frozen. She wasn't wearing her coat. The family grew concerned now seeing her injuries. She was an excellent actress.

In Italian she begged, "I'm so sorry. I don't know what happened..." She whimpered pitifully and let the scene play out like she knew it would.

"Oh no! Come inside, Miss."

The man put his arm around her and led her inside to his wife. He shut the door not knowing his family's fate was sealed.

Lipstick glided over her full lips leaving them blood red. Rebecca checked her reflection in the gilded mirror in her bedroom to find no evidence of the past hour. Her disposition much improved, she was ready to rejoin the party.

A light tap on her door took her attention. Muffled by the door she heard, "Rebecca, are you alright?"

She recognized the lilting French accent of her dearest friend, Collette.

Rebecca walked toward the door and opened it to reveal her friend's concerned face, framed by black hair loosely piled atop her head in a stylish bun. Her diminutive stature was in stark comparison to Rebecca. Rebecca's stilettoes provided an even larger gap in height between them. Collette was more of a ballet flats as dress shoes type of woman. She resembled a wood nymph in a green ethereal looking short strapless dress and gold shimmering flats.

Collette reached out her arms and Rebecca immediately accepted her embrace.

"I know it's hard," Collette consoled.

"It is much harder than I expected." Rebecca conceded.

"I'm so sorry, ma choupette. It's going to work out. You know as well as I do, we have all the time in the world." Collette pulled back but did not release her. "Fucking men," she shook her head and pretended to spit.

Rebecca appreciated Collette's undying loyalty. She looked down at her friend's pert little face, expressing the attitude of a much larger woman.

"That's what I love about you, you're always on my side."

"Of course I am. Fuck him. He wants to play human. It's ridiculous. He'll learn they age and he won't. We have a couple centuries on the boy. I think, if we think back we probably had the same growing pains. It's not you're fault, but after a few years he'll understand the only home one of us can make is with our own. If he expects you to be waiting for him in a decade..."Collette scoffs disgusted.

There's nothing better than having a girlfriend side with you, and Rebecca was more than appreciative. She wrapped her arm around her and squeezed.

"Let's go toast a Grappa to another year well lived. Flavio's brought a case for each of us from his estate in Veneto," Collette said and led Rebecca down the corridor toward the sounds of merriment.

Before they could make it to the end of the hallway, Collette made a frustrated sound and stopped. With a grimace on her face she said, "I was also coming to tell you something that you need to be aware of before you come back to the party..."

"What is it?" Rebecca asked, dread lacing her tone.

"Adam's not at home alone for Christmas."

The statement hung in the air.

"What are you talking about? Tell me!" Rebecca demanded.

"He was tagged in a picture on IG. Several people inside the party have already seen it." Collette explained. "I didn't want you to go in there and be blindsided."

"Let me see it." Rebecca crushed her words through clenched teeth.

Collette reluctantly pulled out her phone and clicked to her last text exchange with a mutual friend. A screenshot that included a picture with a caption was above the text message, "Who is Adam with? He was just tagged in this! Does Rebecca know?! "

Rebecca snatched the phone and studied the picture. Her eyes glinted in the reflection of the phone light as her eyes moved swiftly around the screen. Her mind raced with the possibilities.

The caption read, "Merry Christmas! Hope everyone is having a great night. My house is full. We're making merry and drinking mules!"

The picture was of a kitchen filled with people enjoying themselves where everyone was holding up a glass. It was taken as a selfie of a woman but included everyone behind her in the room. Rebecca's eyes zeroed in on Adam's face. The happy look in his eyes seared through her like a branding iron. Her heart pumped a painful beat and her breathing shallowed.

What the hell is this? How could he be smiling that smile in a room full of strangers? Rebecca's thoughts cascaded.

What she noticed next made her suck in her breath through her teeth in a hiss. Adam was scrunched down beside the woman to be able to be in the picture at her height, one hand holding up an icy glass in cheers and the other hand resting on the woman's shoulder. His fingers seemed to be caressing her. The room was full of other people in the background with various stages of smiles or laughter, with two toddlers running out of frame.

"What the fuck?" Rebecca whispered.

"I know. It's weird. I hate to show you, but letting you go out there would have made me an awful friend. I love you and I'm so sorry." Collette gushed out. Her face cringed.

"I just saw him a couple weeks ago. He said nothing. I was in his house. There was no evidence of anyone else being there. The only scent in the house was his. How the fuck is he part of some family's Christmas?"

"I don't know," Collette said. "Do you think he's with

that woman?"

Rebecca knew in her gut that hand on her shoulder was not an accident or just a gesture. Adam wasn't a man to have his hands on a woman just out of nowhere. He didn't touch any of their friends in any unsolicited way. He wasn't a man to hug too long or brush against a woman untowardly. That hand on her shoulder was there because he felt comfortable with her. Rebecca's stomach tightened at the thought. The fresh blood in her stomach rolled, threatening to paint the walls. Her eyes piqued.

"No. I will not cry in front of anyone." She said and breathed out hard.

"We can deal with this when we get back to The States. I'm there for you, whatever you need of me." Collette promised.

Rebecca straightened her spine and tossed back her shoulders. Her facial features returned to a neutral position with the expertise of an Oscar award winner.

"I'm ready. Let's join the party." Rebecca smiled, but her brain was boiling with thoughts of Adam's betrayal. Her embarrassment in front of her peers would eat her from the inside out but she would never let a soul see it.

"We can deal with this tomorrow."

"Yes we can." Collette smiled devilishly.

They walked toward the sounds of revelry.

Chapter Twenty-four

Sweat trickled into Sara's left eye, blurring her vision. She took her hand off the heart-monitoring sensor on the stationary bike to wipe it. That made the stinging worse and she squinted against the uncomfortable feeling. Even through blurry squinting eyes she could still make out the figure walking up to her left. She huffed a breath and pursed her lips, not missing a beat, her legs still pumping at the same pace.

"We really have nothing to talk about." Sara said to Steve before he could even speak.

She had been dreading the day they would run into each other, but she refused to quit. It was the only gym in her neighborhood. She was on a fitness roll. He was the scumbag and she wasn't going to hand over the place to him.

"I'm so sorry. I'm not a cheater, I swear. Like I said in my texts my wife and I—"

Sara raised her hand, "It's cool, Steve. Well not actually cool, but no need to explain. It's none of my business."

"If I could take you out again, I could explain. My wife and I are separating. Her parents didn't know." Steve smoothly explained like a professional politician, his hands palm up in a gesture of innocence.

"No need man. Seriously, I read the texts. I'm just not

interested anymore."

Sara pumped her legs harder. She hoped he'd get moving and leave her to her work out.

No such luck.

"We could be really good together. If you know what I mean? I know you haven't gotten to really get your feet wet out there dating. I could help you navigate new territory. A fun practice..." Steve trailed off suggestively. He ran his hand through his full head of hair, disheveling it slightly in now what seemed to Sara as a calculated vain gesture to look sexy.

Yuck. Sara shook her head, *this guy is so full of himself.*

She smirked and decided to shock him. "You know that built Uber driver? I practiced 'dating' on him that night, if you know what I mean? I was thoroughly satisfied. So, I'm good."

His face was priceless. She couldn't wait to tell Adam.

While Steve sputtered, Sara continued. "I'm not going to stop coming to this gym, but I would like to never have to talk to you again. Can you just walk past me in the future? Completely ignore me because I will be ignoring you." Sara looked forward, dismissing him.

"I'll be waiting if you change you mind," Steve stated and walked away.

Rebecca's teeth came together with an audible clank when she heard Sara mention the built Uber driver. She'd watched Sara for over 30 minutes before Steve had walked up to her.

Rebecca was across the gym from Sara, jogging on a treadmill looking like a Nike commercial. Her loose bun, perfectly messy the way only models know the secret to achieving. Every male in the gym was aware of her presence. Rebecca's eyes stayed focused on Sara.

She snarled the name in her head.

Sara. Who the fuck is this Sara?

So far, Rebecca had gathered nothing particularly noteworthy about her. She was pretty but aging, while Rebecca remained permanently twenty-seven years old and stunningly beautiful. Rebecca ran down the inventory of how she was better in every possible way. Every possible way that mattered to someone like Rebecca.

Rebecca sneered, disgusted when Sara's face reddened from the effort of working out and sweat began to drip off her face. Wet spots had formed on the fabric of the t-shirt she had on, down her chest and armpits. It made Rebecca sick inside that this was what had replaced her.

When the fit older man walked up to Sara, it boggled her mind.

Another handsome man under her spell. Is she a witch?

The conversation that followed shed a little light on her relationship with Adam. If she was telling the truth, they were sleeping together. Rebecca still had no idea for how long or how serious it could be.

She watched as Sara wiped her sweaty palms on her yoga pants and grabbed her phone. Was she texting Adam? The smile on her face said, yes. Sara typed for a hot minute then chuckled softly before hitting send.

Less than a minute passed and Sara's phone chimed. She eagerly read the message and a loud giggle escaped her lips before her hand came up to stifle it. Rebecca's eyes tensed, focusing on every detail of this woman and her joyful little laugh at a joke sent by Adam.

No.

Was all she thought. Just no.

Rebecca shook her head. She would not take this lying down. A plan began to formulate. She would not stand for losing her man to this old fucking bitch. Rebecca refused to see the irony in that thought.

She watched as Sara stopped her bike and gathered her things. Rebecca waited a few moments before she stopped her treadmill and followed her.

Sara stepped into the sauna, relieved not to see Steve inside. She could overheat in peace. She was still smiling to herself over Adam's texts.

How in the hell do I get along so well with a twenty-four-year-old? She asked herself for the millionth time.

She sat down across from the door and settled in for the sweet, hot torture. Her thoughts drifted, as they seemed to do every other minute, back to Adam. Christmas Eve felt so good and she had longed for him every day since. She had to be responsible. But if she'd been twenty something, she would have dropped everything to spend every minute with him. The butterflies in her stomach from his touch. The warmth of his smile. The deep sexy tone of his voice reverberated in her mind.

Sara sighed loudly.

The door cracked open and a beautiful woman walked in. Sara was taken aback.

Damn. She's fucking hot.

The goddess woman smiled the sweetest smile. "Oh thank goodness. I was afraid the sauna would be filled with men all hairy and sweaty... and too friendly." The bubbly voice was cute and coming out of such a beautiful face was enchanting. Sara was awestruck.

"Today is your lucky day, it's just me. Maybe too friendly and sweaty but only slightly hairy." Sara responded with her kind smile.

She'd seen the woman around the gym this morning, there was no missing a body like that. Sara wasn't too stubborn to admit she hadn't expected her to be so nice. It actually made her a little nervous that she'd be alone with someone so obviously on a higher societal level. Twenty-something with a rocking body, impeccable expensive gym wear and that perfect messy bun.

How do pretty girls get their hair to do that? Would it be weird to ask? Sara thought.

"Well I'm relieved. I'm Becky by the way." She closed the door behind her and sat down opposite Sara. "I'm new here."

"I'm Sara and I would shake your hand but it would be gross for you."

"Is it normal... I mean have you noticed the men who go here are a little..." It seemed like she was trying to be polite by trailing off.

Sara supplied, "too friendly."

"Yes. A guy approached me today to explain how to use a machine I was already successfully using. I've been to gyms before." She gestured to herself indicating, *obviously*. "What was his name... Steve. I was like thanks for the mansplaining. He kept 'helping' me as I went about my own business. Then I saw that same guy bothering you out there. I rolled my eyes so hard. It was obvious you already knew how to ride the stationary bicycle but I bet he had to give you advice."

Sara laughed at her assumption, "Oh yeah, Steve. I was new to the gym a couple weeks ago and he asked me out on a date and being that I was hoping to find a man, I said yes. Come to find out while on the date, he is married." Sara put up her hands and raised her eyebrows. "I hadn't seen him since. He was just trying to explain himself to me."

"OMG. No." Becky seemed aghast.

Rebecca had a limited amount of time to engage with Sara. Sunrise was upon them. She could feel the urge to escape to safety rising in her body. In less than thirty minutes she needed to be inside her blacked out Land Rover. The sauna was also public and they could be interrupted at any moment.

Her features still schooled in the expression of friendly disbelief, Rebecca continued. "Seriously? That guy has some balls. Yuck. Well, I hope your search for a man gets better from here on out."

Rebecca hoped she'd take the bait and continue leaking information.

"It's not going too bad... now." Sara shyly bragged.

Rebecca knew she had her. It's so easy to lead humans. She almost rolled her eyes. Almost. No one could play roles like Rebecca. She could be whoever she wanted you to believe she was.

"Ooh la la. That sounds promising. Are you using an app I need to know about? I'm new in town."

"Oh, you're way too hot for an app. Your inbox would be flooded with di—" Sara stopped herself.

Rebecca saw the slight change in her skin, a reddening flush. Sara must be embarrassed that she almost said something off-color to a stranger.

"Were you going to say dick pics?" Rebecca let out a musical laugh. "You're probably right! How many have you gotten?"

Sara's sigh of relief was evidence to Rebecca that she'd put her back at ease.

"Well, it wasn't through an app, but I was put on the spot recently to give a man at a bar my number. He immediately sent me one. It was my first."

She noticed the sweat beading on Sara's forehead. She could hear her heart increase in rhythm to compensate for the extreme temperature. Thick blood was loudly chugging inside Sara's veins. The smell of her overwhelmed Rebecca's senses for a moment and the urge to drain her dry and snap her neck was like a runaway freight train.

"Is that who 'it's not going too bad' with?" Rebecca questioned.

If Adam sent this woman a dick pic, she didn't know if she could remain in control. Unbeknownst to Sara, her life hung in the balance of her answer to this question.

"Oh god, no! I met a younger man... and I'm kinda freaking out." Sara blurted out. She took a deep breath of hot air.

Rebecca relaxed her jaw. Now this was the information she was after. Her control was fraying, but she knew any information she could get out of Sara could be all she needed. She couldn't kill her today and she knew it. She had a plan. Sara's sudden death, after everyone knew she'd seen that photo at Christmas, would be damning. No one would believe she wasn't responsible.

"Now we're talking. Younger man, huh?"

Rebecca's performance was flawless. She played up

the congeniality in her voice and expression. Her eyes only sparkled with socially acceptable interest. Nowhere in sight was the complete malice in her heart.

"I'm thirty-nine almost forty. You're gonna think this is weird…. Everyone's probably thinking what the hell? He's twenty-four." Sara's face reflected the expression of throwing out a dark secret to a friend and waiting for their reaction.

Rebecca's realization at that point kept her silent for a moment too long. This woman was Adam's real age.

That's what he's doing. Trying out a woman his own age.

"Wow. It sounded worse when I just said that to a stranger out loud. I must be insane to even be contemplating dating a man his age." Sara's expression was crestfallen. She looked genuinely upset.

Rebecca ran through her response options and what they could gain her.

"I didn't mean to make you feel like I was judging. I hope when I'm your age I can be as brave. Have your fun while you still can." Rebecca let the implication that time would be running out for sexual escapades with younger men. "I don't know how you handle sitting in this heat."

Sara sat crestfallen.

Rebecca wiped nonexistent sweat from her brow, stood up and cordially said, "I think I'm going to have to beg out early. I wasn't hydrated enough to do this today. Nice to meet you and good luck with the boy." She let the word 'boy' hang in the air and headed for the door. She quickly opened it and left.

Rebecca had the information she needed. She knew a few minutes more smelling Sara's heated blood in the rage she was in, she might just throw everything away. She enjoyed the fantasy of Sara's lifeless body for a moment. The endearingly sweet expression her face had been wearing faded, revealing the face of a lethal woman.

Sara stepped out of the gym's shower wrapped in a fluffy towel. Her flip-flops forlornly clapped on the tile floor as she dragged her feet to her locker. Her face reflected the downward spiral of her thoughts. She walked by a bay of mirrors and looked over into her eyes and huffed at herself.

Beautiful Becky definitely thought I had lost my damn mind, Sara thought angrily.

"I'm pretty sure she's right," she whispered to herself.

Sara's brain had been in overdrive ever since that young woman's response to her confession had knocked the wind out of her. All she had done was tell her their age difference. She cringed to imagine if she'd explained that not only was Adam fifteen years younger, he also had the face of a movie star and the body of a god. Sara mimicked putting a gun to her head and pulling the trigger.

"Shit."

Sara shook her head and opened her locker. She quickly dried off and redressed in the clothes she'd worn to work the night before.

Adam was coming over tonight for their sleepover. Up until ten minutes ago she had been on cloud nine about it. Just thinking about what she planned on doing to that man, made pressure build between her legs. Now she felt like a fool. An old fool.

Did you see Becky's tight body? She didn't have a single line in her face. That's the kind of woman a man like Adam could date. You've only been working out for three weeks. *You don't think you're in shape do you?* The mean girl in her mind let loose.

I'm trying my best. I have a good personality. She pouted out her bottom lip.

A good personality? You're stupid to believe a twenty-four year old muscle jacked hottie wouldn't be looking at your every flaw.

Sara yanked her gym bag over her shoulder. Her eyes tightened around unshed tears. She was thankful the locker room was empty this morning. She was about to throw a full-blown pity party. Those are best celebrated alone.

"Pull it together, you can cry in the car."

Chapter Twenty-Five

Adam knew the freezer was empty, but he opened it anyway. It was, as expected, completely bare. His stockpile of blood was gone, save for the last bag that was heating up in his towel warmer.

Fuck.

He was in a bind. Anyone that could have helped him had been out of the country celebrating the holidays. His preoccupation with Sara hadn't helped him plan ahead. By the time he knew he needed to break down and ask for help no one was in the states to ask. He had tried to ration after it dawned on him how screwed he was. He was days away from being bailed out of this mess but after draining the last bag he was going to have to starve or beg Raphael to cut his holiday short.

Or call Rebecca.

Fuck no. I'd rather starve.

TV shows and movies show vampires breaking into the Red Cross and hospitals for donated blood, as if it were a cakewalk to commit a robbery. As though every building didn't have 24-hour surveillance. Maybe the police wouldn't find him if he wore a mask and did it a state over, but his community of vampires would spot him right away. The Elders would quickly end him for bringing unwanted attention to their existence.

Adam did not have access to a Volunteer. A Volunteer was what the vampires called humans in the inner circle who were properly vetted. In today's world where everyone can take pictures or videos, you could be recorded at any time. Volunteers signed iron clad non-disclosure agreements and knew that the penalty of breaking it was not just a hefty fee, but their life. The Elders drilled it into everyone's head. Someone posts a video of you doing things only vampires can do and you better run and hide.

Vampires had a system in place, but it wasn't cheap. A month's supply of Volunteer blood would set you back ten thousand dollars. The cost was a stumbling block for Adam at the moment. Trying to live an honest life didn't leave him with a large cache of cash. He had spent everything he'd saved for this last supply. He had stretched out the one-month supply for the last three months.

Volunteers weren't slaves held captive in a basement somewhere being drained. They were perspective vampires. They could also be generational familiars, meaning their families came from a lineage of servants. The whole servant thing had gone out of style in this century for most humans unless you were extremely wealthy, but it was still going strong in vampire culture. Working for vampires had its perks. In today's day and age, job security, living wages, and the intriguing nature of being an insider is worth sticking with.

There was a black market that supplied blood for half the price but the thought of where it might be coming from made him shudder. He'd once accepted a bag of questionable origin and the taste of fear, disease and heroin in it still haunted him.

There are subtle notes that can be tasted in blood. Like a snapshot of someone's life at the moment it's taken from their body. You can tell if they were happy or sad, healthy or sickly, vibrant or depressed. He'd been groomed on Volunteer blood from happy hosts. Tasting fear and pain didn't interest him like he knew it did some of the others.

Rebecca for one preferred the taste of fear. He remembered finding her secret stash. He had never suspected she was unsatisfied with Volunteer blood. It was a decade later when he started seeing the clues that there was a hidden side to her that was actually frighteningly sadistic.

He had been thoroughly disgusted to smell the bags tinged with the adrenaline of a body in shock and fear. Adam had confronted her to only be shamed for not understanding her time as vampire before the modern age. What did he expect from her? At least she wasn't killing anyone anymore. How much more could we expect her to change her ways? It took a few more years to figure out she had never stopped killing for blood.

The towel warmer dinged and Adam took the warm bundle out and unwrapped his last meager supper. He looked forlornly at the empty fridge and freezer.

I'll figure it out tomorrow. I'll have to call Raphael, he thought begrudgingly.

The massive castle door slammed shut behind Rebecca after she quickly entered her home, shutting out the first rays of morning sun.

Sara. Sara. Sara.

The name echoed inside her skull. She stopped walking and just stood letting the encounter at the gym replay. Now she knew why Adam would be dating an aging human woman, but it was still disgusting. The image of Sara's reddened face sweat beading on her brow. The smell of human sweat had permeated the air. She could still smell it. She had been replaced by *that*. She should have killed her right there. Drank her hot blood and tasted her fear.

Stupid old bitch! Rebecca was too livid to recognize the irony of that thought.

"I was getting worried." Collette interrupted Rebecca's dark thoughts.

"I met her."

Collette didn't need any further explanation. She knew Rebecca had been stalking Sara for the past couple days. Her eyes lit up in expectation of the new information in this drama that was unfolding.

"Let's sit. I need to get comfortable for this."

Collette led Rebecca to the sitting room across the foyer. They walked under the massive chandelier dripping with crystals. The new day brought the crystals to life. The room sparkled with ever increasing rainbow prisms.

The sitting room was beautifully appointed. Collette indicated to Rebecca to take the chaise lounge. It was covered in buttery red leather, the focal point of the seating arrangement. Rebecca floated down onto the chaise like a queen. She settled against the overstuffed reclined back and put her feet up.

"Did she survive?" Collette asked and settled into the ornately carved antique chair nearby.

"Unfortunately." Rebecca dryly responded. She looked over at her friend's eager face. "I hate living in today's world. What would we have done fifty years ago... even twenty-five years ago?"

"Bitch would be dead." Collette smirked.

"Exactly."

"It has been hard to adjust." Collette pondered. "It takes a lot more planning to go undetected, to do nothing... untoward."

Untoward was putting it mildly. They had lived centuries as hedonistic killers. Human life meant nothing. Humans were food. Delicious, life-sustaining, orgasmic-level food. They had hunted together during the times before forensic evidence. Rebecca and Collette believed they had lived through the glory days.

Things changed during the twentieth century. They had spent countless hours lamenting about the good ole days for the past several decades. This was no new conversation.

"What are you going to do?" Collette asked.

"I want her dead." Rebecca's voice was made of steel.

"That's going to be a hard one. You would be the only suspect."

"These modern times have put a damper on our freedom, but they have also made us more cunning. I want to glutton myself on her blood. I want Adam to suffer like he has made me suffer. Then I want to kill him, too." Rebecca ended very matter of fact.

"There's the Rebecca I know and love. Over the last few decades, I thought you'd adapted. Gone soft on me. Adam was such a humanly vampire. No one that's been changed in this century is worth a damn. They are so in tune with who they are as a person and invested in their fellow man. J'en ai jusque-là!" So disgusted she reverted back to her native tongue.

"I gave him everything. Everything a human could ever wish for." Rebecca stated. "Power, money, immortality and me. Men have fought and died to be granted my attention. He threw it away like it was trash. Like I was trash. He took my gifts willingly, told me he loved me. How could you turn your back so easily on someone you love? He is a liar. If he thinks he can now happily live the immortal life I gave him..."

Rebecca quickly ran through several scenarios in her head. Each one flawed in some way. Adam had become beloved by their circle of friends. He was like a pet to them. Even after fifteen years he still seemed fresh and new. They enjoyed his company. She had made a mistake turning him. She'd fallen for his charm. She had been taken in by his beautiful face and body. The sex had been phenomenal. Showing up with him on her arm at any given occasion had made her feel like a queen. She reveled in the jealousy of others. Now she knew she was a laughing stock.

"This will take immaculate planning. The Elders can't suspect. Our friends can't suspect." Collette said.

Rebecca looked into her dearest friend's eyes. They were filled with deadly intent and she had never been more thankful for anything in her life.

Chapter Twenty-Six

Sara checked her reflection for the twentieth time. She leaned in and turned her face side to side.

"Hmmm," She nodded. "Not bad."

Not Beautiful Becky either. Her inner mean girl wouldn't let her just have a win.

"Whatever," she whispered to the mirror. "I'm the one getting laid."

The natural excitement of anticipated great sex had lifted her out of the funk she'd fallen into early that morning.

"Beautiful Becky can fuck off."

She stuck her tongue out at the mirror and turned away.

Adam was due to arrive any minute. She walked in a nervous circle, unable to function. They needed to have a talk. She wanted to be flippant about this sexcapade, but she knew herself. She was becoming way too involved and some boundaries needed to be set.

Sara had figured it all out today. Adam was going to be her good friend. They got along so well. Obviously they were cultivating a friendship. She'd had some fanciful thoughts about him over the past weeks, but she'd brought herself back to reality today. She knew she wasn't going to have a relationship with a twenty-four-year-old man, but they definitely were on the way to a friendship that had some damn good benefits.

She planned to lockdown and define what was happening as two adults with similar interests developing a friendship. He couldn't be her boyfriend. That would be illogical. They were in two different stages in life. He should be finding a girlfriend he could marry and start a family with some day. Her stomach clenched at that thought. She wouldn't hold him back from that when he found someone. She would let him go and treasure the memories of their affair. What a lucky woman that would be, to build a life and family with a man like him.

It can't be me. That time has passed. Sara sighed sadly.

Sara heard his car pull up into the driveway. Her heart skipped a beat. She headed for the front door on bouncing feet. The butterflies had migrated back to her stomach. She knew they had a lot to discuss tonight, but there was plenty of time for that. She took a deep breath and opened the door.

Sara gasped as she was lifted off her feet, before she had a chance to say a word.

Adam's hot mouth covered her open lips. His body slammed against hers as he carried her back inside and kicked the door shut behind him. Carnal electricity sparked as his mouth slanted over hers, suckling at her tongue.

He never broke stride as he stomped down the hall that he knew led to her bedroom. He broke the kiss only long enough to look for which doorway he needed to enter.

Sara's heart heated up as if stoked by coal. A steam engine chugging in her chest. The anticipation for what he'd do next sent shockwaves toward her belly. She could feel her heart beating between her legs.

Their lips firmly locked, he lowered her onto the bed and melted himself on top of her. Adam concluded the epic kiss by suckling her lower lip softly as he released her face. Her head fell back against the pillow.

Adam stayed on top of her. A solid wall of muscle holding her down. She felt helpless, yet completely safe. The kiss had ended, but she was breathing like she'd just run the hundred-meter dash. He leaned up on his arms and watched her.

Sara's brain was lit up like a sparkler on the Fourth of July. She finally opened her eyes.

"Well, hello." Sara drawled. "Quite the greeting."

"What can I say, I'm happy to see you." He emphasized the word 'happy' by pressing his hot bulge into her thigh and raising his eyebrow.

Sara giggled.

Adam smiled down at her. His charming smile only for her. Sara stared back at him in wonder. He was everything any woman would ever want in a man and he was in her bedroom. She wanted to wrap her arms around him and never let him go.

What is happening to me?

I'm falling in love with this man.

Adam watched intently as her eyes changed from pools of warmth and delight to sheer panic. He immediately rolled to her side afraid he had hurt her in some way.

"What? What's wrong?" The concern in his voice palpable.

Sara's breathing became erratic.

He grabbed her face when she tried to look away.

"Tell me!" His deep voice demanded.

"I can't." She whispered.

"You will." He demanded. "What's going on inside your head?"

"I can't do this."

"Why? Tell me what just happened in a blink of an eye. I need to know." His eyes were beginning to panic themselves.

"I think I'm falling in love with you and I can't let that happen," Sara whispered with her eyes closed. A tear seeped through her thick black lashes. "We have to stop see- "

Adam knew he couldn't let this conversation continue. He interrupted her words with his lips, shutting her up. He felt her hands push against his chest but he didn't stop his gentle assault on her mouth. She turned her face away and he used his hands on the sides of her face to pull her mouth back toward his. He knew if he could ignite her passion again, he could make love to her one more time, and she would find it that much harder to resist her feelings for him.

Sara softened beneath him and she began to return his kiss. Her hands stopped pushing his chest and started to move over his shoulders to bring him back down fully covering her. Relief flooded through him.

Adam put his hands through her hair as he slanted his mouth over hers, tasting her fully. He needed her love, her warmth. He needed to feel her humanity in his life. He remembered his human life so much more clearly when he was with her. He remembered what it felt like to be in a family. Memories of his life, growing up watching his dad love his mom, had been brought into focus. He couldn't lose Sara and lose that part of himself again.

Sara's hands felt like butterfly wings fluttering up and

down his back. He needed her. She was his connection to humanity. She would keep him sane. The loneliness that was smothering him was gone and now he could breathe.

Adam ended the kiss with several sound kisses to her lips. He deftly turned onto his back pulling her on top of him spreading her legs to either side of him.

"Do you want me?" Adam asked, his voice low and graveled. The double meaning his questions evident to her.

"Of course." Sara breathed.

"Then take me." Adam stated.

A look of uncertainty crossed Sara's face.

"Please." Adam whispered with earnest need.

He watched her make up her mind. She rose up astride him and began to unbutton his shirt. The heat of her pussy scorched his cock through their jeans. His erection strained against her.

Sara knew what she wanted, as illogical as it was. She wanted him. She wanted to say, 'fuck society standards. I want this man to be mine.' She wanted to wake up with him every day. She wanted to watch movies with him every night. She wanted to curl up in his lap after a bad day. She wanted to be fucked by him on the regular. Why couldn't she just take him? What would it hurt to try?

I could end up with my heart broken.

Yeah. So what. It would be worth it.

Maybe it would be.

Fuck it.

You only live once!

She finished unbuttoning his shirt and spread it wide to reveal the curves and planes of his sculpted body. She bit her lip and sighed.

"I'll take you." She said and smiled deviously.

Adam's eyes glinted with devilish delight.

Sara practically purred as she stroked his chest and abs. She bent over to kiss a path from his neck to his hard, beaded nipple. Playfully, she suckled it before licking her way to the other one, giving it the same attention. She nipped lightly at his nipple. She felt him jolt beneath her.

Sara suddenly sat up and said, "Get naked."

While he struggled to free himself from his shirt, Sara leaned across him and opened the drawer to her bedside table to reveal her condoms and a few of her festive looking vibrating friends. Adam leaned with her to investigate.

She pushed him back down and scooted further down his legs to expose his jean covered erection. Sara rubbed her hand on the hot mound before unbuckling his belt. It was like knowing you were unwrapping your favorite toy on Christmas morning. She gleefully unzipped and pulled down his pants and underwear. His cock sprang free and she almost clapped her hands in excitement.

Sara bent over his impressive thickness and breathed softly onto him before pulling it into her mouth with her tongue. He bucked beneath her and moaned. She encircled his cock with her hand and let go of it with her mouth, only long enough to look him in the eye and spit on his dick to lubricate her hand movements. His green eyes sparked fire at her. She moved her fist up and down his cock. His shimmering eyes shut and his head fell back against the pillows.

His broad head filled her mouth completely. He sucked in his breath loudly and tensed under her. Sara reveled in her new found sexual power. She was a goddess weaving a spell around them. She had never experienced this level of decadent desire. She took him deeper into her mouth before suctioning the tip and releasing. He let out his held breath.

"Get your pants off. I need you inside me now!" Sara hastily removed her own shirt revealing a black lace demi cup bra. She left it on. She rolled to the side to kick off her shoes and remove her jeans and panties while Adam pulled off his pants just as quickly. She heard him rummage through her drawer.

Good boy, she thought.

Sara turned back to Adam and pushed him hard to return him to his back. He raised his eyebrow at her and laid back.

"I've been dreaming of riding you." Sara said as she straddled him.

"Ride me, cowgirl." Adam replied.

Sara reached her hand between them and grabbed his cock. She slowly enveloped him with her hot creamy sheath. When he filled her to the hilt she paused and looked down at him. His thumb rubbed her nipple through the lace of her bra.

"Damn. This feels so good." Sara whispered. She ran her hands up his chest. His skin was heated steel. His muscles flexed under her touch. She slowly lifted herself, feeling every inch of his wide girth. She gave herself over to the throbbing pleasure between her legs. The pressure intensifying as she quickened the pace.

Adam placed his other hand right above where their bodies were joined creating a firmer landing pad for her clit to hit every time their bodies smacked together. She moaned and threw her head back, riding him with sheer abandon.

"Fuck! YES!" Sara yelled to the ceiling.

"Are you going to come for me?" Adam's deep voice

was low and strained.

"Yes!"

Sara's heart was sputtering an erratic beat. She rode him hard, squeezing her muscles as she was bucked by him. The sparklers in her belly were burning white hot. She knew she was close. She closed her eyes and held her breath focusing on her climax. She stopped moving. Adam drove himself into her. She flexed all the muscles in and around her core. Her clit contracted and seconds passed in blissful suspension before it throbbed her release through her entire body. Adam had paused his thrusts to let her focus on her orgasm. When she melted down onto him, he grabbed her hips and thrust himself into her, pounding until he found his own release.

Sara felt like a rag doll draped onto his chest. The rise and fall of his chest under her face felt heavenly. They both remained silent, letting themselves drift back down to Earth.

Sara didn't want to think about the words she had spoken earlier, 'I think I'm falling in love with you.' Had she really said that out loud? Yes. Those words had been spoken and there was no way to take it back. She contemplated what she could possibly say now.

Adam played with her hair. It cascaded over his belly and down his side. He relished the simple human enjoyment of the light touch from her soft hair on his skin. He ran his fingers through it, lifting a lock, twirling it and putting it back down.

'I think I'm falling in love with you.' He replayed those words. If he could break down her resistance, he knew she could love him.

But will she love you when she finds out about you? He asked himself.

That was the question that kept him up during the day. How could he possibly ever tell her his secret? It would sound insane to her. She would probably laugh. Think it was joke. She would definitely question his mental stability. He would have to prove it to her and then what? She'd be appalled.

He had worked through hundreds of scenarios over the past couple weeks. It wasn't something he was going to tackle tonight but the thoughts remained close to the surface of his mind at all times.

"All my clothes survived this time." Sara mumbled against his chest.

Adam chuckled, his chest bouncing her face up and down.

She rose up to look at him. Her hair wildly disheveled, fell forward becoming curtains on each side of their faces. The smell of her shampoo lingered in the air between them. Honeysuckle and something earthy he couldn't put his finger on.

"What should we do now?" Sara asked.

"Whatever you want?" He replied.

She cocked her head to one side and click her tongue, "Ummm, I'm starving now."

Adam smiled up at her while he let his hands roam around to her backside. He gave her a quick spank and said, "Worked up an appetite, huh?"

Chapter Twenty-Seven

"Cheers," Sara said as she held up her hard cider bottle.

"Cheers," Adam responded clinking his bottle of beer against hers.

They both took long drags and set them down at the same time. The table was covered with take out that had just been delivered. They had plated up and now it was time to dig in.

"I can't wait for you to try these. They are the best tacos in town and I've done the leg work." Sara picked up her delicious looking street taco and sank her teeth into it. She chewed while making appreciative noises.

Adam followed suit and after a couple chews gave her *the look*. You know the look where the food was so good it just blew your mind.

"Right?!" Sara exclaimed after she swallowed.

Adam nodded agreement and continued chewing.

They enjoyed their tacos in silent reverence. Sara couldn't stop looking at him. He was beautiful. His sharp jaw flexing with each bite. Tacos and a sexy man after having mind-blowing sex. She was riding high.

I won the lottery, she thought nodding her head.

"What has you grinning?" Adam said shaking his head.

"I was just counting my blessings this evening." She replied.

"Me too. Great sex, beautiful woman, tacos and beer." Adam said raising his bottle. "I couldn't ask for anything more."

"You read my mind!" Sara laughed.

"What are you doing for New Year's?" Adam asked.

Sara was caught off guard. Even though they were enjoying each other, she didn't expect he would want to spend New Year's with her. She had secretly wished for it, but she hadn't wanted to put him on the spot. She still didn't understand how or why he would want to spend important holidays with her. Kissing him at midnight danced though her mind. She felt her whole body sigh.

"It's okay if you've already got plans. No pressure." Adam tried to backtrack.

"No, it's not that. I am just surprised," Sara responded peeling the label on her bottle nervously.

"Surprised at what?"

"Surprised that you would want to, I guess. I have barely processed the fact that you seem to want to hang out with me at all."

Sara looked away embarrassed. She had told herself she wouldn't bring up the disparity in their age tonight.

As if that's the only disparity, Sara thought and frowned.

Nothing booze won't help me forget.

She raised her bottle to her lips.

"Sara, will you be my girlfriend and kiss me at midnight on New Year's Eve?"

"What?!" Sara choked on her cider.

Adam waited silently for her to recover.

"Are you serious?" She said as soon as her airway and mental capacity had cleared.

"Dead." Adam replied.

Sara looked at him. He was masculinity and youth. His virility permeated the air around him. His size and presence in the room overwhelmed her for a moment. She leaned back in her chair, her breath wooshed out of her.

"I don't know what to say," Sara began.

He stayed silent and still.

"Why? Tell me why you want me? I don't understand. I've been going along with this because I'm the one that benefits the most from being with you. You are in the prime of your life. I'm not. I'm just taking advantage of your interest while I have it, but I can't imagine that I will have it long."

"I do look twenty-four, that's true. I can't help that, but that's not who I am. I'm just a man, who has been living a lonely life lately. I grew up in a warm and loving home. Honestly, I've been adrift. You came into my life like a beacon of light. You live a life of joy and laughter. You're a beautiful woman. Yes, I'm well aware you're thirty-nine. That's not the definition of who you are either." Adam took her hand in his and repeated. "Will you be my girlfriend and kiss me at midnight on New Year's Eve?"

"Adam... I don't..." Sara stumbled, her insecurities screaming. It was one thing to boast in her head that she was cool enough to date a twenty-four-year-old man but to really do it. She wanted to run for the hills.

"I remember what you said to me in your bed." Adam stated. "Do you need me to remind you?"

"No. I remember." Sara's face lit up with embarrassment. She could kick herself. Her penchant for blurting out awkward truths always got her into trouble.

"I feel the same way." Adam said.

Sara's mouth dropped open. Was this conversation really happening? She gawked at him unable to respond.

"I have never felt this way about a woman before. I've had more fun with you in the short period I've known you than I've ever had with any girlfriend. Loving you would be easy."

Sara closed her gaping mouth. Her heart thumped in her ears almost as loudly as her own thoughts.

"I want us to be exclusive." Adam continued.

Sara tried to organize her scattered thoughts. She remained silent until she saw a change in Adam's eyes. His eyes became uncertain and a slight change in expression crossed his face. His hopeful expression faltered and sadness entered his eyes. That was her undoing.

"Yes." Sara whispered barely audible.

"What was that?" Adam cupped his ear pretending he needed assistance hearing her. "I mean you don't have to, if it's going to be a burden on you..." He stood up suddenly and swept her out of her seat and high into his arms.

Sara let out a surprised squeal. One second she was seated, the next she was cradled like a baby. He easily maneuvered her like she weighed nothing. Sara's brain couldn't quite comprehend how that was possible.

"I'm gonna need you to speak into my good ear." Adam declared as he angled her face directly beside his left ear.

"All right. All right. I guess I'll be your girlfriend." Sara pretended to reluctantly concede.

Adam let out a low rumbling belly laugh as he pretended to toss her in the air. Sara gasped in surprise. Her joyous laughter joined his. Smiling from ear to ear, she wrapped her arms around his neck and held on tight.

"You're crazy!" Sara said breathless.

Adam kissed her forehead in response, but didn't put her down.

"All I want to do is Netflix and chill with my new girlfriend. Is that so crazy?"

"Is that *all* you want to do?" Sara asked suggestively.

"What more could I ask for?" He asked feigning ignorance.

Sara lightly grazed the back of his neck with her fingernails. "Oh I see, you're spent for the night. I'm sorry. I understand if you won't be able to get hard again. It's a common problem."

Adam gasped overdramatically, playing into her joke.

"Are you doubting my manly abilities?"

"Oh, honey. It's all right. Even if you could get hard, I doubt you'd be able to come again... I mean I bet you couldn't make me come again so soon either. Yeah, let's go... Netflix and chill."

"You doubt we could come again, huh?" He raised an arched brow. His eyes danced with delight.

Adam put Sara on her feet and grabbed both her hands in one of his, easily trapping her. He leaned forward, towering over her. His other hand slipped into her hair, gently wrapping a large portion of it around his fist. His eyes playful, but his grip firm.

"You know what happens to ladies who question a man's virility?" He said in a deep macho voice.

"I'm hoping he's forced to prove his manhood by fucking her brains out," Sara laughed. She loved that he was playing along, and that they could tease each other so brazenly.

Adam released her hair and replied, "You guessed right."

He walked past her still holding both her hands in one of his. She was forced to jog to keep up with him as she followed him back to her bedroom. She couldn't help but giggle the entire way.

Leading a giggling woman to bed was pure, unadulterated fun. Adam was thoroughly enjoying this sleepover. He reached the bed with Sara in tow. He schooled his features back to macho tough guy and turned back to her.

"If you knew what was good for you, you'd be begging for me to take it easy on you." He said as he pulled her to him.

"Please Mister, don't be too hard on me. I'm a delicate flower. I've never done this before" Sara responded in a sickly sweet and innocent tone.

Adam almost laughed but kept his features serious, "Oh my. We have a virgin on our hands. Do you need an experienced manly man like me to show the way?"

"Only a manly man like you could deflower a delicate princess like me."

"I'm going to deflower the fuck out of you. Get naked."

"As you wish, Mister Manly Man." Sara grinned and threw off her clothes in record time.

Adam stripped down as well.

"I guess you can get hard twice in one night." Sara deviously winked at him as she ran a finger down his solid rod. Switching back to her virginal voice, "It's so big. I don't know if it will fit."

Adam shook his head and rolled his eyes at her. He loved her silliness. This playful banter was exactly what he wanted. A life filled with joyful laughter.

"It's mandatory for the virgin to say that to the experienced macho man. According to every romance novel I've ever read." Sara grinned. "Did it make you feel like a dominant alpha manly beast?"

Adam grabbed her wrists in one of his hands, "Would you like me to be a dominant alpha manly beast?" Adam lowered his voice to gravel.

"Well, for one thing, an alpha manly beast wouldn't ask," Sara joked, feigning disappointment.

"Damn it."

Adam pulled her toward him putting her arms around his waist. Her pebbled nipples grazed the skin of his chest. He swayed back and forth against them, relishing in the simple pleasure. "I've got to work on that."

Sara's hands kneaded his backside as she looked up at him. The need he saw in her cerulean eyes sent blood pounding south to his cock, throbbing between them. He inhaled, taking in every nuance of her scent. The smell of her arousal made his cock strain against her hot, soft skin. He listened to her heart trilling out an erratic beat. The thought of drinking her hot oxytocin tinged blood, made his mouth water. For a moment he imagined fucking her while tasting the sweet thick, nectar.

Too many days had gone by with only half rations of blood and today he only had the one bag left. It wasn't enough.

If only I could...

He had let himself get to a state of thirst he hadn't

reached before. He knew he needed to curtail this line of thought immediately.

"What are you thinking?" Sara asked interrupting his effort to gain control of his burning thirst.

"Contemplating my next manly move."

Adam winked and swallowed hard before regaining control of his wayward thoughts. He trailed his fingers along the sides of her face and into her hair, brushing it back behind her ears.

Adam tilted her head exposing her neck. Sara's wildly throbbing pulse was visible under her skin. A shock of bloodthirst exploded throughout his body. His mouth watered and his nerve endings caught fire. He lowered his head, not exactly sure what he planned to do next.

I have to find a way to focus on fucking and not on sucking! He inwardly smirked at his play on words.

Adam trailed kisses along her neck and felt her shiver in his arms.

"Let's find out what makes you scream?" Adam whispered into her ear.

Sara's response to that was nearly a purr as she melted into him.

Adam picked her up and deposited her into the middle of the bed. He quickly rummaged through her bedside table and spotted the vibrator she had stashed between her bed and the table. This one he knew had to be her go-to stimulation device. He grabbed it, threw it on the bed next to her and she grinned at him. Adam gave her a knowing look and a wink.

He quickly followed her and laid beside her on his side. Adam leaned over her to kiss her, toying with her tongue until she was squirming with need. She wrapped her arms around him, pulled him closer and meshed her body against his. She threw a leg over his and firmly pushed her hot core against his thigh. Her soft moans filled the air.

Adam ended the kiss. He kept his thigh between her legs rhythmically moving it against her as he pushed her onto her back and moved to cover her with his body. Her head fell back on the pillow and her breathing came in short bursts.

Adam pulled his thigh up tight against her. Her pussy scorched his skin. She was so ready for him. He was so ready to sink deep into her, but he wanted to draw this out and make her desperate for fulfillment.

"Let's just fuck," Sara stated, out of breath.

"Oh no. I told you I wanted to see what makes you scream." Adam shook his head before he took her nipple into his mouth and suckled. She ground her wet slit into his rock-hard, muscled thigh. His cock throbbed in rhythm with the bucking on his thigh.

"Please." She begged desperately.

"I think you may be getting too close. We can't have that." Adam removed his thigh from between her legs. She groaned with disappointment.

"You devil." Sara whispered.

He drew her nipple deep into his mouth and pinched the other one hard enough to get her attention.

Sara arched her back and whimpered in ecstasy. Adam let go of both nipples and kissed a trail up to her mouth. They shared a long drugging kiss before Adam expertly flipped her over onto her belly. She let out a surprised yelp.

The lovely curve of her sweet ass beckoned him. He leaned over and kissed the small depressions where her back met her bottom.

"I love these dimples," Adam said before kissing the

other one. "Did you know they are called The Dimples of Venus?"

"How about you use them for gripping and get behind me," Sara demanded as she started to rise up on her knees.

"Oh, I will, but not yet."

Adam loved this. He pushed her flat against the mattress. She made a frustrated sound that made him laugh out loud.

"First, I need to give this ass some attention."

He gave a quick love tap on one of her plump cheeks, testing the waters. Her pleasured moan muffled by her pillow was the answer he was hoping for. He kissed the spot where his hand had been. He continued to lick and nibble down to where her leg and cheek meet.

Sara writhed beneath him, stoking the fire in his hardened dick. He leaned back and spanked the other cheek slightly harder than his test run.

"Adam!" She screamed into her pillow, her breathing labored.

"Yes, love?" He whispered before giving this cheek the same loving attention as the other one. Her restless movements beneath his tender assault drove him wild. She tried to rise up again to entice him to mount her. This time it worked.

Adam got to his knees and spread her legs to either side of him. He positioned himself behind her, his cock jutting out straight as a spear to meet her soaking wet pussy. He grabbed her hips, his thumbs on the cute indentations he'd kissed earlier, and pulled her back. He slowly pushed his thick, throbbing cock into her welcoming sheath. He withdrew slowly, his bulbous head pulling against her opening but not letting himself exit her. She greedily backed up on him and he met her with a strong thrust.

"Oh my god!" Sara exclaimed. "That dick Yes!"

He lifted one hand from her hips and swiped it down in a stinging spank. Adam drove into her with controlled force again and again. Sara grabbed her vibrator. It came to life with a deep buzz. She held it to her clit and moaned appreciatively.

Adam growled out his climax at the same time Sara screamed hers into her pillow. They collapsed in a pile of spent heavy breathing. He rolled to the side so as not to crush her. She stayed face down, but slung her vibrator off the side of the bed.

Sara turned her head his way and said, "You fuck like a much older man."

That hit too close to home.

"What makes you say that?" Adam asked curiously.

"You just know how to fuck." She sighed. "I haven't had sex with any twenty-four-year olds since I was twenty-four, but as I recall they didn't do it as well as you do. Not by a long shot. "

Chapter Twenty-Eight

"Did you bring pajamas?" Sara asked as she rummaged through her dresser drawers and came out with soft fleece pajama pants and a lacy tank top she had purchased specifically for tonight's sleepover. She wanted to look effortlessly cute and comfortable. She put them on, relishing the decadent coziness. She walked to the closet and pulled out a thin peached-jersey leopard print half robe.

"I didn't think of it. I was preoccupied imagining the sex." Adam responded.

Adam was sprawled out on the bed with his hands behind his head, looking very satisfied with himself. Sara stared at him while she secured the ties of her robe around her waist. His feet were almost hanging off the end of the bed. His long, muscular legs looked sculpted out of stone. When he lifted his head up to look back at her, his abs flexed and Sara bit her lip. A tinge of desire shot down from her stomach.

Sara was surprised at how easily he turned her on after already being thoroughly satisfied. Well, maybe she wasn't surprised.

Shit, my pussy is going to be sore tomorrow.

Her smile widened.

"You want to watch a movie now?" Adam asked.

"Have I serviced you enough my queen?"

"Hmmmm, for now my lowly man slave. For now. I bought tons of snack foods and ice cream. Let's get this party started!" Sara chirped. She picked up his discarded clothes and threw them on top of him. "I'm going to get snacks going," She said over her shoulder as she walked out of the room.

Sara skipped down her hallway and let herself do a twirl or two.

He likes me. I think he really likes me!

She stopped in the foyer and hugged herself and sighed.

I can't believe this is happening.

Sara replayed their earlier conversation. He said he felt the same. That he was falling in love with her, too. There wasn't an inkling of deception about him. She thought she should probably be skeptical, but being skeptical sucked. She wanted to believe him.

"Take that, Beautiful Becky!" She whispered.

Adam surprised her wrapping his arms around her from behind and putting his chin on top of her head. "Who's Beautiful Becky?"

Sara, a bit startled by his stealthy approach said, "Oh this amazing looking woman at the gym this morning. You know the type: effortless messy bun, twenty something, eyes like I've never seen before... like amber. She made me question myself after we had a conversation in the sauna."

Adam went completely still. His arms tightened around Sara. It couldn't be, but he knew it had to be.

"What did she say?" Adam demanded.

He tried to keep the alarm out of his voice as his mind reeled with the information that his Sara had been alone with Rebecca with no one to protect her. She had been completely vulnerable and now he knew she was at any given moment. What was Rebecca planning? Why would she seek Sara out this way?

Sara turned around in his tight embrace and pushed against him.

"I'm sure she didn't mean to hurt my feelings she seemed really nice. Why are you looking so weird?"

Adam forced himself to soften both his grip and his features. He sniffed the air deeply. Rebecca knew how to find her. She could be here now. He let his hearing reach out to the neighborhood. Were they being watched right now?

How could he have let himself be so immersed in their time together that he wasn't keeping vigilant watch of their surroundings?

"Adam. What is going on in your head? Your eyes are a little crazy right now." Sara questioned.

He smelled the threat before he heard it. His nostrils flared. Then, a small creak on the front porch followed by a knock.

"I could tell it was time to make my move. Don't even try to run."

The voice, one only Adam could hear, spoke from the other side of the door. Another knock, this time louder than before.

Adam couldn't believe this was happening.

He recognized the voice. It was Collette, Rebecca's best friend. She would do anything for Rebecca. They had spent centuries together and were more like sisters.

Why would she be here? Was Rebecca here as well?

He turned his head listening for any other sounds around the house.

"Adam, I need to see who that is. Let go."

Sara's confused voice cut through his panicked haze.

"Yes, Adam. You need to calm down and act normal. We can sort this out." Again, Collette spoke softly on the other side of the door, and only his ears could hear her.

"I don't want anyone to *have* to get hurt..."

Adam knew he was fucked. He let his arms drop from Sara. He couldn't outrun Collette. He'd been barely sustaining himself on blood. She would catch them before they could get out of the backyard. In fact, Rebecca could already be waiting out there. Sara would scream. Neighbors would call the police. They would all die.

He had to find out what Collette wanted. If it was to stop seeing Sara, he would to keep her safe. His heart cracked at the thought. If Rebecca was angry enough to have Collette here, he would find a way to bargain with her to leave them alone. Maybe this was just some plot to scare Sara off. Not a really mature course of action for Rebecca to undertake, but a woman scorned, they always say. He could get through that. Sara wouldn't be in danger if that was their plan.

Sara opened the front door to reveal Collette dressed in jeans, tennis shoes and a high school sweatshirt. She was in her early twenties when she was turned and being as short as she was, passed easily for a teenager. She smiled up at Sara, wide eyed and innocent.

"Hey, I'm sorry to bother you guys, is Hazel here? I popped my tire on a curb up the street and my phone's dead... I knew she lives here. My dad is going to be so mad at me!" Collette perfectly impersonated the cadence of a young, insecure teen in need of help. Sara's Achilles Heel if there ever was one. She rubbed her arms and bounced as the wind blew by her into the house.

A tendril of icy fear crept up Adam's spine. They know who Hazel is and that was a clear message to him that he needed to play along for her safety as well as Sara's. He'd never felt such dread before in his life. He almost choked on it.

"Oh honey! Come in. It's freezing!"

Sara had invited her in.

Adam stopped breathing.

"You poor thing. My cell is in the kitchen, I'll go get it." Sara stepped aside letting the teen pass by her.

Poor little thing, she thought. Sara remembered a similar incident she'd gotten herself into when she was sixteen. Back before cellphones, and having to knock on a stranger's door at two AM for help. Sara, lost in the memory, didn't notice the newcomer had closed and locked the door behind her. Which should have seemed quite odd.

"There will be no need for that."

Startled by the voice that now came from the pixie sized girl, Sara looked at her. She no longer slouched, her voice was clear and confident. She looked Sara straight in the eye. She had thick raven hair and her eyes were an odd gray. Almost silver with chips of diamonds that made them gleam. They pierced through Sara with a confident malice that took her breath away.

Sara was utterly confused. She looked back at Adam and he looked like someone had stunned him. His eyes sparked with what bordered on desperation and it made absolutely no sense to her.

Sara tried to take a step back to get a hold of what was becoming a completely baffling situation. Who was this girl? What is Adam's problem?

She was stopped by the girl's small hand on her wrist. Sara looked down at it. She'd never felt anything like the grip of this hand encircling her wrist. She puzzled at it. The strength of it was otherworldly.

"Hey, what..." Sara couldn't go on as she tried to pull her hand away and it didn't move a millimeter. The confusion in her brain was now being clouded with pure fear. How is this girl holding her this way and why?

"Collette, stop! What is your game?!"

Adam's deep, iron laced voice broke through Sara's bewilderment. She heard his fear and adrenaline shot through her system almost buckling her legs. He called her Collette. He knew her.

"Adam!" Sara still uselessly tugged at her wrist. How could she not pull away from such a small girl? Her brain could come up with nothing to explain this.

Collette breathed in deeply through her nose and smiled, "Do you smell that Adam? That first shot of straight fear dumped right into the bloodstream?"

"Why are you here? Did Rebecca send you? Let Sara go and I'll go with you to work this out. Whatever you want? Just leave Sara alone. Please!"

"Oh Adam, so naïve." Collette smirked at him. "She doesn't know what you are, does she?"

"No." Adam sounded defeated.

Sara looked into his eyes questioning him.

"What you are?" She whispered.

Sara stopped trying to pull her arm away. It was

obviously completely futile and she needed to focus on what was happening. Who this Collette was and why she seemed to be a danger to them. What was wrong with Adam? Why he was not trying to gain control of this Collette. She was maybe five feet tall and a woman. Adam being six foot four and completely jacked, why wasn't he just picking her up... Too many thoughts cascaded into her mind.

Adam remained silent.

Collette laughed and said, "Oh this is everything. Rebecca will be so sorry she missed it. She's on an airplane. We couldn't have her anywhere near this, but she will be quite jealous of how delicious this is... and will be."

"Collette, why are you doing this? I've known you for fifteen years. I thought we were friends?" Adam said desperately. His mind raced with possibilities. What had they planned and what could he do to get Sara out of this?

"Oh honey. I've known Rebecca for three hundred years. You are nothing and will be nothing very shortly. You're just a mistake Rebecca would like to forget."

Collette moved forward, easily dragging Sara along. Sara's eyes were wide, surely that remark about three hundred years was blowing her mind. Adam clenched his teeth. He would die in a fair fight with Collette. He readied himself, watching the scene for any vulnerability. He knew now that they weren't meant to survive this plot and he needed to figure out a way to save Sara's life.

"How do you think you can get away with this? Everyone will know it was Rebecca's doing." Adam desperately needed more information to find a way out.

"Adam, what is happening?" Sara demanded, her fear

palpable.

"Yeah Adam, what is happening?" Collette mocked. "Explain yourself to this *food* you're fucking."

"Sara, it's going to be all right. I'm so sorry. This is all my fault. I just wanted a normal life-"

Collette cut him off, "Shut up, Adam. Go ahead and move ahead of me very slowly to that bedroom that was just rocking. We can set a scene there. Don't even think about trying anything. I can make this very drawn out and filled with unimaginable pain."

Collette pulled Sara along indicating for Adam to take the lead to the hallway.

Sara panicked. Like a wildcat, she fought and pulled at her wrist. Adam's head spun. His drive to protect Sara was killing him, but he knew he was no match for Collette and watching Sara's fear filled face wrenched a knife in his gut.

He hadn't fed fully in months. The thought of feeding on Sara and then being able to defeat this bitch flew through his mind. The many consequences of that also flew by. Collette could kill her in an instant and would he ever get a chance to make that move.

That would be the end of the relationship.

Who am I kidding? This fucking situation is the end of this relationship.

Adam's heart clenched like a stone in his chest. He looked deep into Sara's eyes. A tear had escaped. She was looking at him for help that he couldn't give her right now. Her struggles were getting her nowhere. She reminded him of a gnat buzzing around the face of a lion. His stone heart became a boulder in his chest. He almost doubled over.

Adam knew he needed to keep Collette talking. She was so sure of herself. She had already given him the information of Rebecca's involvement. He took a deep breath and steeled himself.

"So what, Rebecca's on a plane? You don't think the Elders won't automatically think of you?"

"Why would they? When it will be so obvious what's happened here." She stated cryptically.

"What *is* going to happen here?" Adam demanded at the entrance to Sara's bedroom. He stopped in the doorway and turned to face Collette. He contemplated fighting her.

Collette poked him in the chest with her index finger. He hadn't expected the blow. He found himself sprawled out in the middle of the floor instantly. He heard Sara's gasp at the display of power from Collette's slight form.

"What are you?" Sara screamed at Collette.

"Bitch, I think you mean what are *we?*"

She pulled Sara through the door and closed it behind her.

Chapter Twenty-Nine

Sara stood in the middle of her bedroom. The one in which she had just shared in pure bliss with Adam. Only ten minutes earlier, she had been falling in love in this room, with the man that now was splayed out on the floor looking utterly defeated. How had that small woman's touch sent him flying?

The events of the past couple minutes were unbelievable and made no logical sense. Time was moving slowly. She had been dragged into this room for what? Adam knew this woman and someone named, Rebecca.

Rebecca. The moment she'd said the name Becky, Adam had gone weird. That's when this started. Like she had said the magic word and now she was in Hell. Collette had known Rebecca for three hundred years. Was she joking? The display of inhuman power, that defied every bit of Sara's logic, made it a possibility.

I'm going crazy, that makes knowing someone for three hundred years a possibility?!

I'm in the fucking Twilight Zone.

"Sara."

Adam's tortured whisper broke through her panic. "You'll be okay. I'll find a way. You mean everything to me. I'm so sorry."

"Don't get your hopes up, he can't win. He's weak. He

hasn't fed like he should have in months."

Fed? What the fuck does that mean?

Collette put a delicate foot down onto Adam's arm and pressed. Adam screamed in agony as she smiled. He tried to push her away with his other hand, but she barely swayed.

"Stop! Don't hurt him! What do you want?!" Sara's stomach rolled. The sight of his pain sent tears streaming down her face.

Collette turned her silver gaze to Sara and picked up her foot. Adam's howl stopped. He rolled over quickly to put some space between them before jumping up to his feet.

"I can't fight her like this, Sara." Adam whispered his eyes filled with sorrow.

"Have you guessed yet?" Collette quipped cheerfully.

"Guessed what?" Sara responded.

Collette rolled her eyes, "What we are? Your new boyfriend has been keeping a little secret. Bad boy." She sat down on the bed, completely relaxed. "What drinks blood and fucks your brains out?"

"Drinks blood?" Sara whispered.

"Yes, ma cherie. We drink blood. Have you ever seen Adam during the day? Think, you ape. He's a vampire. But Adam here wanted to live a human life and throw away everything Rebecca gave him. Can you believe that? How ungrateful. You know Rebecca, you met her this morning. Yes, she and Adam used to be a thing. I think it's safe to say Rebecca's over you. Or will be after I'm finished here."

"Vampire." Sara said the word in shock. "No. There's no such thing."

Sara looked at Adam, her eyes filling with questions and disbelief. His eyes were hardened, filled with determination. Sara couldn't imagine what he was thinking. His jaw was set in a hard line and his eyes seemed to be begging her, but for what?

"He does fuck like a much older man." Collette mocked Sara's earlier private statement. "I was listening outside to everything. It was very entertaining."

"Why?" Sara needed an explanation. "Just leave us alone." She pleaded.

Adam was slowly inching closer to Sara's side. Sara couldn't look in his eyes any longer. She looked to Collette. Panic was giving her tunnel vision. Everything about Collette was hyper focused. Everything else in the room was a blur. She sat on Sara's bed her legs up and crossed. To any casual observer, she would look like a friend ready to gossip.

"I was waiting for the perfect time to interrupt your evening, but when you mentioned meeting Rebecca, I knew the jig was up. I sure as shit didn't want to give Adam time to get to his phone and text any friends of ours."

"How will you explain this?!" Adam's steely voice demanded.

"Oh all right. I'll play the blabbermouth villain. I see why they do that now. It prolongs the moment. I mean a villain could just do whatever it is they were going to do and explain nothing but then there would be no relishing of the moment."

Collette was carrying on so nonchalantly about the fact that she was here to hurt them, Sara thought she must have fallen into another dimension. How could any of this be happening? Hot tears scorched her eyes when she thought of Hazel's face. The beautiful life she'd lived as Hazel's mother flashed before her eyes. She had to survive this. She had to find a way to fight.

Fuck this bitch. She thought.

Sara looked back to Adam who was now slightly closer than the last time she made eye contact with him, his masculine features so otherworldly in their perfection. She would have never imagined they actually were supernatural, but now she could see it clearly. He was too strong. Too handsome. Too everything. A vampire.

What the fuck?

Sara was brought back to the moment when Collette continued.

"Adam hasn't been taking care of his needs. You see he's poor. Can't afford the rations of blood needed. He's been stretching out his supply. Rebecca noticed the last time she was inside your home that your supply was dangerously low. She knew you didn't have the cash to restock. So... we knew you'd be in a weakened state. That it would be easy to kill you. Come to find out you're as weak as a baby and have no chance at all to save yourself or Ms. Cougar over there."

Adam growled, "You still haven't explained how you expect to get away with this. Our friends aren't stupid."

"They know you were a cuddled little modern vampire bitch who has never feasted direct from the source. You don't know what it does to you. How you won't want to stop. And how easy it is to *accidentally* kill the first delicate human you drink from. In a moment of passion you give in to temptation and devour your new woman friend. Overcome with guilt you kill yourself. Voila!"

"Shit." Sara whispered. "Adam?"

She had to admit it sounded like a good plan. The news of her impeding demise made her knees weak.

Sara looked up at him. He looked like a predator. Every sense keen and alert. His eyes so laser-focused on

Collette's every move. He looked ready to pounce. From what Sara had witnessed earlier, he would lose. He would die.

Sara's chest tightened and her breath escaped in harsh expulsions. Her mind raced for any possible escape from this.

"I need you both naked for this set up, so take off your clothes." Collette leapt off the bed like a jaguar and was next to Sara in an instant. "You sounded like you've really been enjoying this hunk. Let's recreate the scene."

Collette reached out and brushed Sara's hair behind her ear as if they were lovers. The bizarre dichotomy of gruesome intentions and the gentle touch made her cringe back in revulsion.

Adam grabbed Sara from behind and pulled her away from Collette. Tightly held against him in a protective embrace, Sara almost felt safe.

Collette laughed, "Oh Adam, you're so cute."

He squeezed Sara and said evenly with intention, "I won't lose control."

Sara got the message. She'd already weighed every possibility. There was no way to run. No way to fight. The only way out was to trust in Adam. She tilted her head exposing her neck to him.

Sara's consent granted. Adam knew this was their only chance. He had one shot at taking control of this situation and killing Collette. His sharp incisors elongated. It disgusted him that his mouth began watering in this dire situation. He was about to put Sara's life in the balance.

The instant he lowered his head, Collette rushed toward him. The advantage to being 6'4" was the wingspan. He stopped her at arm's length at the exact moment his teeth penetrated the warm silk of Sara's skin. He turned his body away from Collette keeping Sara as far away from her as possible. Protect her or die trying. His arm bent from the pressure Collette was exerting to reach them.

Sara's gasp filled his ears.

Blood filled his mouth.

Collette screamed in indignation as she pushed against his hand. At her size, she looked like an angry child being held away from him. Adam's large hand gripped her throat. She kicked and swung at him. She dug her feet into the floor and tried to push closer. His arm bent further. Her hands were within inches of his body. Saving Sara gave him the extra determination he needed. His arm was on fire. Every ounce of his will focused through it.

The hot sweet nectar poured forth from Sara and Adam eagerly locked onto her and sucked it down. This was beyond anything he'd experienced. Fresh and life sustaining, he could feel his starved cells rejoicing as they assimilated the bounty. His heart pumped wildly in his chest. He gulped greedily letting the power roll through him. It heated him from the inside out, licking his every molecule with flame.

Collette doubled down on her efforts. The floor creaked under the pressure. Like a Mack truck against his arm, it buckled further. Her hands tore away his shirt, but thankfully could not catch his skin. She changed tactics and seemed intent on breaking the arm holding her back. She raised both feet and drop kicked him in the side. She held onto his arm and used her feet to climb up his body. She kicked his ribs mercilessly.

Adam focused on stoking the blaze inside him. He was strong when he was turned. He knew he was stronger than Collette fully blooded. He was the strongest vampire he knew. He hadn't met anyone else turned at the peak physical condition that he had been at twenty-four.

He swallowed another mouthful of Sara. Velvet ribbons of blood flowed down his throat. He could feel her pulse on his lips. With each pump of her heart his thirst was being quenched. Her life-force was fueling him. The ecstasy of doing exactly what a vampire was made to do was intoxicating. This felt too good. He didn't want to stop.

Can I stop?

Sara's whimper broke through the violent whirlpool of his thoughts.

The damage he was sustaining to his ribs and arm was brutal. The sound of cracking bones filled the room. Despite the pain, he remained steadfast. Torrents of life-sustaining energy vibrated through his body. Every muscle tingled as if coming to life.

He swallowed one last time and raised his head from Sara's neck. He kissed the two wounds there and swiped his tongue over them. Cleaning the blood that oozed from the punctures. He unceremoniously tossed Sara, across the room, hopefully to land on her feet but he couldn't be certain. He needed her as far away from Collette as possible.

"Put pressure on it!" He shouted to her and focused completely on subduing Collette.

Collette had destroyed the right side of his torso with her feet. He was lucky his hand had remained tightly closed around her neck. The crushing pressure of her grip finally broke through his resistance and his arm gave way.

The sound and view of Adam's arm breaking was too much for Sara. She couldn't control her gag reflex. She leaned over and heaved her dinner onto the floor beside where she had landed hard on her ass. Tears streamed down her cheeks. She held her hand against the wounds on her neck. It stung badly and blood oozed between her fingers. The thought of it made her gag again. What if she bled to death?

Did he puncture anything major?

Collette turned her attention toward Sara, fury sparking from her eyes. In a blur, Adam grabbed the locks of her hair that trailed behind her. It stopped her progression toward Sara in its tracks. The look of disbelief in her eyes was almost comical.

Adam was stronger now. He practically glowed with vitality. The look in Collette's eyes as he pulled her back was evident. She knew it, too. Sara watched as indecision flickered across her face. In an instant, Collette raised her hand and ripped her own hair out of her head, releasing her from Adam's grasp.

She was gone. Her hair hadn't even landed on the floor, when the front door slammed shut.

"Fucking shit!" Sara's mind reeled as she struggled to stand without touching the pile of vomit beside her. She felt lightheaded. The room swirled around her.

Everything went dim.

Then black.

Chapter Thirty

Adam was torn. Should he chase after Collette and try to murder her back? He couldn't even believe he had to contemplate such a thing. Sara was face down, unconscious beside a pile of vomit. He worried he had taken too much of her blood. His arm was bent the wrong way. It radiated a pain beyond anything he'd felt in his entire life.

This is one cluster fuck of a nightmare.

It was rather easy to decide; Sara came first. He went to her and knelt down. He carefully lifted her with his good arm and just stood holding her for a minute. She didn't come to, but he could hear the steady beat of her heart. She would live.

The immediate danger was over. He would have to formulate a plan to deal with Rebecca and Collette later. He didn't know if he would bring their friends into this, or try to deal with them directly, but for now the danger had passed. There was no way she would be coming back tonight.

Adam held Sara tighter and breathed a sigh of relief. He had done it. He had defeated the villain and saved the girl. He nodded his head proudly. It felt pretty damn good.

His revelry was short lived however, remembering that Sara now knew what he was and she'd been put in a deadly situation. Her life had been threatened. She wasn't going to

244

just get over it.

He walked to the bed and gently laid her down. She didn't stir at all. She looked disheveled as hell. There was blood smeared down her neck and robe. A few chunks of their taco dinner clung to her hair, along with the smell of vomit that filled the room. He didn't want her to wake up to find herself this way.

I need to clean the scene, He thought.

Adam's ribs hurt like someone had taken a nail gun to them and his arm needed immediate attention. He dreaded it, but he had to reset it so it could heal correctly. He nearly gagged at the thought of it.

Injuries had always grossed him out. He knew it would be all right in a couple of hours. It wouldn't take long to heal. He could already feel the tingling of his skin repairing itself from the places Collette's nails had torn and gouged.

He had to straighten the arm now. He looked down at it reluctantly.

Fuck.

Adam walked to the full-length mirror, removed his shredded shirt and examined his torso and misdirected arm. He was black and blue and there were long gashes down his arm. It looked like special effects in a horror movie. It didn't feel like special effects, though. He wasn't too macho to admit that the pain was making his eyes water.

He grimaced at his reflection and whispered, "Fucking bitch. Jesus. This is going to suck."

Adam knew putting off the inevitable would only prolong the experience. He grabbed his wrist with his good hand and pulled hard. His eyes did more than water. He sucked in his breath through clenched teeth and was able to pull his wrist hard enough to set the bone with a sickening slurp sound.

"FUCK!" Adam yelled in a whisper. He doubled over trying to breathe deep through the waves of shock and pain.

The worst is over. The worst is over, He repeated reassuringly to himself.

He tried to find the most comfortable way to hold his arm, but there was none. He needed to find something to make a sling out of.

Adam opened Sara's closet door and smiled when he saw his shirt. He remembered Sara rushing up her front steps in only this shirt. The epic walk of shame. He put it on gingerly. It smelled like her. Adam rummaged around, found two scarfs and secured his arm in a makeshift sling.

He glanced over to Sara. She still hadn't moved. Her breathing was shallow, but her heart still beat true. Adam set about to right the room and clean up the puke. He found paper towels and cleaning supplies in the kitchen. Luckily, he could hold his breath for long periods of time and got through it without adding to the pile. When the carpet looked sufficiently cleaned, he dared to sniff the air and only the slightest tang of barf remained.

After cleaning the chunks out of Sara's hair, Adam wiped her neck with a warm wet towel. He frowned at the puncture wounds. The skin around them was bruising and the holes seemed deep. One was slightly torn. He should have been gentler.

Yeah, I should have bit through her skin more gently. That would have made this so much better, he thought sarcastically.

He hated he'd done that to her, and also hated how deep down he wished he could do it again. The memory of the rush of euphoria the moment his teeth penetrated and his mouth filled with her hot, thick blood. The exquisite taste only tainted by her fear. The thought of her blood when she was laughing or... coming. That sent his own blood south thickening his cock.

"I'm a monster," he whispered, shaking his head to redirect his line of thinking.

When all the blood was wiped away and the only evidence of foul play were the two clotted holes, he went in search of some Neosporin and bandages. He wondered if she'd be scarred and it made him cringe. She would always be reminded of Collette trying to kill them.

Collette.

The thought of her made his blood boil. He'd been contemplating what the hell he was going to do about her, but hadn't decided on a course of action. He hoped talking it out with Sara would help him make the best choice. If Rebecca was still hell-bent on terrorizing them, her family was in peril and it was all his fault.

Adam sat sentry beside Sara and waited.

Sara came to with a gasp for air and flailing arms. Well, one flailing arm. The other hand was enveloped in Adam's firm warm grip.

"Adam!" Sara exclaimed.

Her mind raced as she replayed the events of the evening. She let go of his hand and put her hands to her neck. Her neck was bandaged. She prodded at the bandage and grimaced at the soreness.

"So that really happened." Sara said hoarsely.

"Yes, that really happened." Adam answered reluctantly. "I'm so sorry."

Sara tried to reconcile all the information flooding her brain.

"You're a vampire. That's a real thing. One tried to kill us because your ex is a total cunt? Seriously?"

Adam smirked at her word choice for Rebecca.

"That about wraps it up."

"Your arm?!"

"It's fine. I almost blew chunks resetting it, but it's going to heal in a few hours."

Speaking of blowing chunks Sara looked to where her pile had been. It was gone.

"You cleaned up my puke?" Sara said awestruck.

"I can hold my breath for a long time. I figured saving it for you to clean up would be pretty shitty of me."

"That's the sweetest thing anyone's ever done for me." Sara gave him a half smile. She couldn't force her mouth to create a whole one.

"You're being very gracious right now. I'm dying over here waiting for the shock to wear off and for you to tell me to get the fuck out."

Adam ran his free hand through his hair.

"I'm so overwhelmed," Sara answered. "Honestly my brain is exploding right now. I have so many questions. I was so scared."

A hot tear slid out of the corner of her eye remembering Collette holding her captive with absolutely no effort. How scared she'd been thinking she was about to die and how Hazel would be devastated. The thought of missing the rest of her daughter's life was too much.

When Adam wrapped his good arm around her Sara broke down. She cried in earnest. Between snorts and sniffs she brokenly rambled, "Seriously, a vampire? I don't know what to think. What does that mean? What am I supposed to do now? You misled me... I've never seen anyone's arm broken in front of me. Her eyes were so cruel... She could have won."

All to which Adam whispered soothing supportive words like, "I know, honey." "Everything will be fine. I'm sorry," and rubbed her back.

Sara's emotional outburst was winding down. She was a little embarrassed. She had clung to Adam while she cried and rubbed snot all over his shirt. She breathed in snubbed breaths and tried to sniff up her snotty nose. She wiped the tears away and rubbed the back of her hand against her dripping nose.

She finally said, "Please don't tell me you're like a hundred-year-old man? Gross." Sara made a face like she'd just tasted a lemon.

Adam snorted a laugh in spite of the serious situation and she giggled in return.

"Are you ever serious?"

He squeezed her and gave her a fake reprimanding shake of his head.

"I can't handle any more seriousness tonight. A vampire tried to murder me. And you have shit taste in women, which makes me question myself as a person. My new boyfriend could be an elderly man." Sara paused. "What else...."

Adam cut her off before anything else could tumble from of her mouth.

"Sara, I will make sure you are safe. I will take this to the Elders. What happened tonight is against everything they are striving to achieve for us as an evolved society. They will take care of Collette and Rebecca. Or I will. I have friends, Sara. None of them will let this stand. Please believe that you are safe now. Your family will be safe. I promise."

Adam couldn't bring himself to ask, but all he wanted to know was if she was planning on breaking up with him after this? It was right on the tip of his tongue, but he was afraid of her answer. Why wasn't she railing against him for lying to her? Why wasn't she calling him a piece of shit for putting her life in danger? He figured she must still be shock. The full scope of the situation hadn't come into focus for her, other than that why was she making little jokes and leaving her hand held in his.

"I can only hope that's true."

Her blues eyes were troubled when she looked deep into his eyes. He knew she was searching for answers. He wondered if she could see inside his soul? He wished she could. She would see that he'd do anything to keep her safe.

"I swear to you, I had no clue something like this could happen. That she would pull this woman scorned bullshit. It's fucking cliché. Rebecca and I broke up a year ago. I can't even fathom what she was thinking sending Collette here. They're from a different time. I've heard stories of the lives they used to get away with living." Adam paused contemplating their lives for centuries.

"How they killed for blood so easily. Our relationship ended when I found out she was still secretly feeding off the unwilling, to put it mildly. I see now that expecting history not to repeat itself was really stupid. But I've never witnessed anything like that from any other vampire. It's no longer how we live and it will not go unpunished."

Sara stayed silent. She looked deep in thought.

"It's killing me to know you could have been hurt or killed. That I might not have been strong enough. If she had gotten her hands on you..." Adam couldn't go on picturing Sara at the mercy of Collette. He imagined the life and joy draining from her eyes forever. The fear he'd felt in those moments was still too fresh. His guts tightened and he clinched his teeth.

Sara placed her hand on the side of his face. "I'm okay."

Adam shook his head. She shouldn't have to be consoling him.

"You're being too easy on me. I put you in danger. Not intentionally, but something like that can't just slide."

"It's not just sliding. I'm trying to process the existence of the supernatural. But also, the thought of breaking this off makes me want to cry. If you left right now and I spent the rest of this night alone, I can't think of anything more horrible."

"Neither can I," Adam said earnestly. "This is not how I wanted you to find out. Honestly, I would have told you. I hadn't figured out how, but I would have. I really am the same guy I was when I was human. I didn't lie about those things. My parents did love each other and my childhood was amazing, filled with memories of their love. I do want that, and I see that happening for me with you." Adam paused and continued with what he hoped would make her smile, "And I'm not an elderly man."

"Oh, that's good to know. How old are you?"

"I'm forty. That's why we have so much in common. We grew up during the same decades." He answered.

"Shit." Sara said flatly.

"What?"

"I'm not a Cougar." Sara replied crestfallen.

Adam grinned.

"I bought all that cheetah print for nothing."

Adam's phone vibrated on the bedside table, startling them both. He forgot about his arm's predicament and reached for it. Pain radiated throughout his body and he tumbled off the side of the bed landing, on his injured side.

"Adam! Are you alright?"

Sara leaned over the bed, a concerned look on her face.

"That was unpleasant."

Adam breathed deeply before he was able to grab the phone with his good arm at the next ring. When he saw who was calling, he sprang to his feet.

"Who is it?" Sara exclaimed surprised by his sudden movement.

"Rebecca," he said, his voice filled with dread. He tapped *answer*.

"You're fucking Face Timing me after what you did?" Adam demanded, every bit of anger evident in his voice. His eyes flamed and nostrils flared.

Rebecca's eyes were calculating. She paused as if deep in thought.

"Have you told anyone yet?" she replied curt and to the point.

"Not yet."

"Then I think we can come to an arrangement."

"Fuck your arrangement! You tried to kill us. Collette was in Sara's house. She was here because of you! You want an arrangement now that it didn't work out? Go to Hell."

"Calm down, Adam. You're so dramatic. Your best choice is keeping this between us. I call a truce."

"Are you kidding me?!"

"Think about it, idiot. If you call in the Elders, I *will* find a way to kill that bitch or her brat kid before they take me. Want to risk it?"

Adam heard Sara's horrified gasp at the mention of Hazel. Rebecca had him. It was true. The moment he told anyone of what Collette had done, everyone in Sara's life would be in danger. He looked back at the phone and saw Rebecca's know-it-all expression.

"You're sick." He growled in frustration.

"I am disappointed in the outcome of the evening. Having to endure this phone call after Collette bungled up a perfectly laid plan." Rebecca shook her head. "But no one else has to be involved and no one else has to get hurt. I'm willing to let you go on with your life. I've already been thoroughly embarrassed by you. We can call it even."

Adam sighed hard. He had no choice, but to agree to this. Rebecca and Collette would get away with attempted murder, but Sara would be safe.

"I want your word. You will not come near Sara or anyone in her family. That you will leave us alone. Permanently."

"I had one shot, it didn't work out, and I can live with it." Rebecca smiled disingenuously. "You won't tell anyone?"

"No." Adam growled.

"Good boy." Rebecca ended the call.

Adam made a guttural sound and threw his phone across the room. It exploded against the wall sending shrapnel all around them.

Sara moved away from him, toward the other side of

the bed. She stared at his heaving chest. He may be a man easy to laugh and gentle of touch, but at this moment he looked dangerous. His height and broadness vibrating in anger was clear evidence of the formidable opponent he could be.

"Adam?" Sara whispered, testing the waters.

Would he lash out at her? He never seemed like a man who would do that, but one never knew.

"She won," he stated flatly.

Sara moved back to the side of the bed where he stood. His stance was firmly planted, his fists tight.

She put a hand on his shoulder and said, "You won. You saved my life."

"The ones that tried to take it will be free, unpunished."

"Yep." It was all Sara could think to respond because that was totally true.

He ran a frustrated hand through his thick hair. "She doesn't deserve to win this."

"She didn't. You did. We are both alive. Lucky for me my boyfriend's a super hero."

"Stop trying to make me feel better." Adam shook his head.

"It's what I do." Sara responded.

"I had to drink your blood, remember? My teeth broke your skin and you might be scarred for life. I don't know. I didn't want to stop. Your blood was like drinking euphoria. I reveled in it. My mouth watered when you submitted yourself to me. I'm not a super hero." Adam said through clenched teeth.

"Submitted myself to you? What? Get out of here with that. I decided to trust you. I'm glad I did! Submitted myself..." Sara was starting to get riled up. He saved the day and now they were safe. Nothing else mattered.

"I said my mouth watered at the thought of drinking your blood, even though our lives hung in the balance, and you're caught up on whether or not you submitted to me?" Adam said incredulous.

"Yeah! I did not *submit*. I'm just making that very clear."

Adam's mouth started to turn up into a smile. "Fine... You didn't submit."

"Thank you. If anything, you submitted to my trust in you," Sara said illogically. She'd turned the conversation around and that always made her happy.

"Now you're stretching." Adam's white teeth flashed in his wide grin. "That makes no sense."

"So. I made you smile and you are sickeningly handsome when you smile."

Sara ran her hand from his shoulder down his back.

"You flatter me."

Adam cupped her cheek and looked her in the eyes.

"I have to know. Do you plan on continuing to see me after all of this... and the being a vampire thing?"

"Dude. I don't think you understand..." Sara said, reading the raw vulnerability in his eyes continued quickly. "The magnitude of the fact, that this right here is many a woman's fantasy. Don't you watch movies?"

"Seriously, Sara?"

"I am serious..."

Sara was struck by a thought triggered by her mention of movies. "Wait! Wait! Adam, I watch movies and read books am I infected?!"

Sara's hands went to her neck, a panic stricken look on

her face.

"No. Calm down." Adam pulled her hands away from her neck and spoke in a soothing deep tone. "That's not how it works. I am not venomous or whatever they've come up with in fiction. Relax. You'll be fine."

"Oh, thank god!" Sara breathed a hard sigh of relief. The shot of new panic scattered her brain. She remained speechless as she shook her head. A shiver of relief gave her goosebumps.

"What? You didn't want to be turned into a Vampire by a guy you just met three weeks ago?" He eyed her knowingly.

Sara loved when he raised one eyebrow that way. It was adorable. She smiled back at him.

"A girl can only take so much in one night." She responded.

A yawn took her by surprise and she swayed a little off balance. She didn't feel like herself. Too many adrenaline spikes. She'd never been in a life-threatening situation before. It had been an exhausting night.

"You should get under the covers and rest. I don't know how much blood you lost. Your dinner is no longer... with you either. I'll get you some water and that ice cream you mentioned. You need to rehydrate."

Adam pulled the covers back with a no-nonsense look on his face.

It did sound like a good idea. She didn't really want to be upright anymore. Sara slid under the covers and snuggled down. It felt good to be taken care of, so she let him fuss over her.

Adam returned shortly with her bowl of ice cream in the crook of his good arm and a big glass of water in his hand. He handed her the water first and waited for her to take a few big gulps. He traded her the ice cream bowl for the glass and set it on the bedside table. She scooted over for him and held up the covers. Adam climbed in fully clothed and settled in beside her.

"I'd offer to play a show on my phone for us but I don't have one anymore," Adam said shaking his head.

"That's okay." Sara said in-between spoonfuls of ice cream.

Exhaustion was catching up with her. Sara's eyes were getting heavier with each bite. There was so much to think about. This beautiful man beside her was a vampire and had saved her life tonight.

He said her blood tasted like euphoria... *What does that even mean?*

Her thoughts became clouded with sleep. She felt Adam take the bowl from her hands and place it on the end table. Sara instinctively nestled herself into Adam's side and drifted off.

The first rays of sunlight woke Sara. She blinked, squinting against the brightness, the events of the night before cascading through her mind.

"Adam! Sunlight!"

She sprang into a seated position. He wasn't in the bed.

A piece of paper lay on his pillow. She snatched it up.

Sara,

I didn't want to wake you, but I needed to be home before sunrise. I won't be able to get a replacement phone until sundown tonight. I can only hope that you wake up still wanting me, because I will never change my mind about wanting you. You've brought joy into my life and there was nothing I needed more.

Love,

Adam

P.S. Looking forward to kissing you at New Year's.

OH and this is our secret, obviously right??? I forgot to say that last night.

Sara clutched the letter to her chest and sighed. She chuckled at the last line.

Yeah, obviously.

My boyfriend's a vampire.

She imagined telling Shawn and snorted at his imaginary reaction. She shook her head. She had wanted to live her life, and this was definitely a once-in-a-lifetime adventure. Falling in love with Adam was only the beginning.

The End

Thank you so much! I hope you enjoyed reading about Sara and Adam falling in love as much as I enjoyed writing it. Soon you can find out what happens next. Until then if you have a moment to leave a review, I would love you forever. Thanks in advance!

If you'd like to stay in the know, find me on Facebook, Instagram and follow my Amazon author profile.

http://www.facebook.com/KathrynVegasAuthor

www.ingramcontent.com/pod-product-compliance
Lightning Source LLC
Chambersburg PA
CBHW021954190626
46807CB00005BB/2249